JUNE SPARROW AND THE MILLION-DOLLAR PENNY

REBECCA CHACE
ILLUSTRATED BY KACEY SCHWARTZ

BALZER + BRAY
An Imprint of HarperCollinsPublishers

Balzer + Bray is an imprint of HarperCollins Publishers.

June Sparrow and the Million-Dollar Penny
Text copyright © 2017 by Rebecca Chace
Illustrations copyright © 2017 by Kacey Schwartz
www.harpercollinschildrens.com

ISBN 978-0-06-246498-9 (trade bdg.)

Typography by Jenna Stempel
17 18 19 20 21 CG/LSCH 10 9 8 7 6 5 4 3 2 1

First Edition

For Rebecca, Ruby, Emma, and Pesha,
best of daughters, best of friends.
And for Ken, who showed me his penny book
and took me to South Dakota.

Contents

1
A Perfect Tragedy

When June Sparrow's eyes popped open that morning, there were eight words ringing in her head: *Today is the best day of the year!* Better than Christmas and better than fireworks. June was turning twelve! She stretched her legs out under the covers and noticed with annoyance that they were the same length as they had been the night before. Then her legs hit a lump followed by a tumble and squeal as something hit the floor. She had forgotten that Indigo Bunting was sleeping at the end of her bed.

Indigo Bunting was June's pet pig. And not just any pig, a miniature pig. He was not only the cutest but also the most intelligent animal on the face of the earth according to June, and Indigo Bunting was far too clever to disagree. He couldn't help being cute because of his diminutive size (he was about the length of June's forearm and weighed four pounds, three and one-half ounces) and extreme cleanliness (some might even call him fussy). Plus, as June liked to point out, everyone knows that pigs are smarter than dogs.

Indigo shook himself, jumped right back up, ran the length of the bed to June's pillow, and gave her a big, snuffling kiss. He hadn't forgotten her birthday.

"Thank you, Indigo," June said, kissing him on the tip of his little pink snout. She picked up the framed photo of her parents on her bedside table and gave them a kiss as well. She always kissed their photo first thing in the morning and last thing before bed. It seemed the least she could do, as they had left her in possession of a very large fortune.

June missed her parents, but they had died when June was only three years old, so she didn't remember them all that well, and June and Indigo were doing just fine on their own.

June Sparrow had no idea that everything was about to change.

That night, June and Indigo had tickets to the opera for her birthday. June did not just enjoy the opera; she adored it. Her mother and father had adored the opera as well, and since they lived in New York City, they were able to go to one of the best opera houses in the world, the Metropolitan Opera, or the Met, as everyone called it. One of June's only memories of her mother was dancing around the living room in her arms before her parents went out. June could remember the feeling of silk against her bare feet as she wrapped her legs around her mother's waist, and the smell of jasmine perfume. Jasmine had been her mother's signature scent, and there was still one small bottle in a velvet box tucked inside the top drawer of her mother's dressing table.

June used a drop or two every now and then for special occasions.

This was certainly a special occasion. For the first time this year, Shirley Rosenbloom, June's housekeeper, allowed June to go alone, or rather, with only Indigo Bunting as her date. Despite what many adults assume, there are some pets that enjoy getting dressed up in miniature versions of human clothes. Indigo Bunting didn't just enjoy getting dressed up—he adored it.

June picked out a silk dress with pink lace along the sleeves and matching pink tulle flaring out below like a petticoat. She pulled it over her head and twirled. Indigo Bunting covered his eyes with his trotters, which was his way of telling her that she looked like she was wearing a Halloween costume.

"You're one to talk," June said, as she fastened the rhinestone clasp on his velvet opera cape and tucked the elastic band for his tiny silk top hat under his chin. June picked up Indigo so that they could admire themselves in the huge mirror by the front door.

"Perfect!" she said. Indigo wriggled in anticipation and made sure that his top hat peeked out proudly from under her arm.

They were headed to their favorite juice bar, Gray's Papaya, for a quick stop on the way to the opera. June weaved her way expertly through the glamorous couples on the street. It was early evening, and the sidewalks were so busy that June pretended that she and Indigo were white-water rafting, leaning into the stream of bodies and breaking through when there was an opening in the crowd, always on the lookout for those annoying people who stopped dead in their tracks to look at their cell phones, creating unexpected boulders in the stream.

"Good evening, Miss June," said the man at the juice bar when they arrived. "The usual?"

"Yes, please!" June settled herself onto one of the tall stools at the counter, put Indigo on the stool next to her, and gave his seat a quick spin. Indigo loved to spin, and he insisted she keep it up until June's tall, frothy papaya juice arrived with a hot dog on the side. (All beef, of course—for obvious reasons, June never ate pork.)

"And this is for your date." The Juice Man cut some papaya into bite-size pieces and put them into a Dixie cup for Indigo Bunting. June gave him a big grin as Indigo tipped his nose into the cup. The Juice Man was not very particular about the "no pets allowed" rule, and after all, the counter was open to the sidewalk. June took a bite of hot dog and sighed happily. Indigo paused in his own gobbling to smile at her. Yes, she thought, taking a sip of juice, this was living.

"Miss Sparrow?" A familiar voice interrupted June just as she slurped (rather loudly) the last of her drink through a bright pink straw.

"Mr. Mendax?" June was shocked to see a slightly built and extremely well dressed man standing at her shoulder. Mr. Mendax was the Chief Financial Officer for her parents' company, and she saw him only once a year, on Christmas Day, when he dropped off a gift basket for June and had a glass of sherry with Shirley Rosenbloom. June wiped a gob of ketchup from the corner of her mouth.

Mr. Mendax looked extremely uncomfortable. In fact, he looked so uncomfortable that June wondered if he was about to throw up. Maybe it was the sight of Indigo Bunting at the counter, eating his meal right beside her, that was making him turn green. Some people had a hard time understanding pigs as pets.

"Happy birthday, Miss Sparrow," said Mr. Mendax, looking even more pale.

"Thank you." June exchanged a glance with Indigo. This was getting weirder and weirder.

"The fact is, Miss Sparrow . . ." He pulled on his shirt cuffs with their tasteful gold cufflinks and looked down at the floor, which was layered with dropped straws and crumpled napkins in a filthy collage of pink and white. "You have no money."

"What?" June spun around on her tall stool. "Of course I do!"

"Do you know much you have?" Mr. Mendax asked.

"Not really," June said, surprised. "You're the one who's supposed to know that, Mr. Mendax."

"No, I mean, how much do you have on you right now?"

June wondered if Mr. Mendax was there because he needed money, despite his fancy suit and gold cufflinks.

"I have"—June opened her purse and unzipped the inside pocket, where she kept a roll of bills— "about a hundred and fifty dollars, but we haven't paid for our snacks yet."

"It will have to do," Mr. Mendax said hurriedly. He pulled out a piece of paper from his breast pocket and handed it to June. It was an airplane ticket in her name to Red Bank, South Dakota. June stared.

"What is this?" she asked.

"A boarding pass." He pressed a large ziplock bag into her hands as well. "And here are some of your mother's personal possessions, from the safe in my office. Nothing of real value. No cash, I'm afraid. Just a few mementos, but I thought you'd like to have them."

June stared at the ziplock bag and the boarding pass.

"What's going on, Mr. Mendax?"

This was the moment when Mr. Mendax burst into tears.

"It was a Ponzi scheme," Mr. Mendax said as he dabbed his cheeks with a paper napkin.

"Ponzi what?" asked June. Mr. Mendax began a very confusing explanation, frequently interrupting himself to sniffle as he wept. He had invested all her money—here, June stopped him: "*All* the money?"

"All of it." He nodded tearfully. "I was going to make you rich."

"But I was *already* rich!"

"I was conned," Mr. Mendax sobbed. "Listen to me, Miss Sparrow. I have only a few minutes before I have to turn myself over to the authorities."

(June had always thought that Mr. Mendax *was* The Authorities.)

"I have spoken to your aunt Bridget, in South Dakota—"

"Aunt Bridget!" June had never met her aunt, though she received a Christmas card every year.

"Your mother's sister is named in the will, should anything happen to me, and now, I'm afraid— something has." Mr. Mendax began to weep copiously. "I will be taken to prison, and you will go to your aunt in South Dakota."

"I will do no such thing!"

"I am so sorry—it's all I can do for you. Please, go directly to the airport." Mr. Mendax glanced out at the street. "You'll have to get a cab there. I—I haven't any money to give you—everything will be sold—even their coin collection—price-less!"

Just then two police officers walked over and took Mr. Mendax rather roughly by the arm. They had been standing at the other end of the counter for quite a while, but June hadn't paid any attention to them.

"Time's up," one of them said, while the other put a pair of handcuffs on Mr. Mendax's slender white wrists.

The first officer finished his shake and left a few bills on the counter. "Tough break, kid," he said to June, and they marched Mr. Mendax out onto the street and into the back of a squad car.

"Don't go home!" Mr. Mendax called out as they were taking him away. "Go straight to the airport. Nothing I can do! Ruin! Bankruptcy! Catastrophe!" He was still sobbing when the policemen shut the door and turned on the siren, speeding away into the night with Mr. Mendax's tearstained face pressed against the window.

2
La Bohème

As soon as the police car sped away, Indigo tugged the boarding pass out of her hand. The plane would be leaving in six hours. Indigo looked very worried, but June Sparrow was not the kind of girl who simply did as she was told.

"Six hours," she said thoughtfully. June asked for the check, and the Juice Man told her it was on the house this time. Under the circumstances, she decided it was the appropriate moment for a gracious thank-you.

Just then, the Juice Man pulled out an enormous bouquet of white roses from under the counter.

"Happy birthday, Miss June," he said.

June was stunned. "How did you know?"

The Juice Man smiled. "I've been making papaya shakes on this corner for a long time, Miss June."

"They're beautiful," June said softly. "Thank you." She jumped down off the stool with her bouquet in one hand and Indigo in the other.

"What should we do, Indigo? Am I really ruined? Should we still go to the opera?" Indigo looked at her long and hard, then pushed his snout into the bouquet and snuffled deeply.

"You're right," June said. "It's still my birthday, and I am not going to spend it at the airport!"

June carried the roses into the opera house with Indigo Bunting hiding behind them. It was perfect camouflage, as pigs weren't technically allowed to attend the opera, and this seemed like the best way to make an entrance. June settled into her box surrounded by white roses with Indigo Bunting on her lap, and as the curtain rose, she thought that if it was really and truly her last night in New York, this was as nearly perfect as it could get.

La Bohème was one of their favorite operas. It was over-the-top romantic: fantastic costumes and arias, bucketfuls of snow falling from the rafters, and the glorious grand finale when the young heroine, Mimi, dies in the arms of her lover, Rodolfo. When the curtain came down, June and Indigo had both soaked their handkerchiefs with satisfying tears for Mimi (and maybe a little for themselves). June thought that she wouldn't mind having a handsome poet mooning over her, but to be perfectly honest, Indigo Bunting was much better company than Rodolfo.

When they stepped outside the opera house, the fountain at Lincoln Center was shooting high bubbles through the beams from the spotlights, and even though she knew they really had to get to the airport, June couldn't help herself—she kicked off her ballet flats and ran around the cement rim of the fountain in her bare feet. Indigo Bunting raced ahead of her. He was small enough to occasionally

throw in a tiny pirouette without falling off the edge. After three times around he was panting hard, and June swept him up and kissed him right between his little pink ears.

"We have to to say good-bye to New York, Indigo!" June said. "We have been dealt a harsh blow by fate." (Going to the opera always made June feel very dramatic.) "But our story is not yet over; in fact, it is only beginning!" Indigo started wiggling his curly tail in agreement. "June Sparrow and Indigo Bunting are as New York as bagels and cream cheese! We're as New York as King Kong and the Empire State Building!"

June put one arm into the air and Indigo wrapped himself around her elbow, baring his teeth and trying to look like an enormous gorilla—he wasn't very convincing, but she knew what he meant.

Suddenly there was the sound of applause, and they looked up, surprised to see that a small crowd had gathered. A woman wearing a feather boa dabbed her eyes, and someone yelled, "You go, girl!"

June picked up her flowers from the Juice Man and threw them out to the crowd like a wedding bouquet. It scattered into a dozen white roses in the air. People scrambled to catch them, and there was more applause.

"Now that's what I call an exit!" June whispered to Indigo as they jumped down from the lip of the fountain.

"There's still two and a half hours before the plane leaves, Indigo," June said when they reached the sidewalk. "I think we have just enough time to go home."

Indigo gave her an incredulous look, but she picked him up and ran. Home was the Dakota. The most fabulous address in all of New York City. The building where Leonard (¡¡*West Side Story*!!) Bernstein had lived. The building where John Lennon had been shot and Yoko Ono still lived. June had never lived anywhere else in her life, and she swore that she never would. As she liked to say to Indigo Bunting, the Dakota *was* opera.

But when June arrived, there were four police

cars with their lights flashing pulled up in front of the building. Antonio, the night doorman, came running out to meet her.

"Miss June"—he was stuttering with anxiety—"don't go in, Miss June. Mr. Mendax said—"

"I know what he said," June said desperately. "I just need five minutes." She glanced at the police cars. "Hold them off, Antonio! Five minutes!"

Antonio stared helplessly as she ran past him into the building and up the stairs to her apartment. Luckily, Shirley Rosenbloom hadn't come home yet from her weekly movie night. Indigo glanced at the hall clock with a worried expression, but June ran straight back to the library. She had almost forgotten her birthday present.

The library was June's favorite room, filled with the comforting smell of old books and lemony furniture polish. There was a fat globe that spun smoothly on its axis and a ladder on wheels that went along a metal railing so that you could reach the books on the top shelf and push yourself around the room. But tonight June didn't have time to zoom around on the ladder. She went straight to the back corner of the library with Indigo trotting behind her, making anxious noises about the time.

Of course, no great library could be complete without a secret door. June removed a copy of *Alice in Wonderland* from the far right bookshelf to reveal a small bronze handle set into the wall. June turned the handle and the bookshelf swung open like a door, into a tiny room with a glass case set upon a small table.

June went straight over to the case and flicked a switch, illuminating it from the inside. She paused for just a moment. Though she had seen it before, this always took her breath away: her parents' priceless coin collection. June didn't know what all these coins were worth, but she knew that this was why they were kept hidden in the secret room. There were gold sovereigns and some very old silver currency from other countries, but rare American coins had been her parents' specialty. Mr. Mendax had been horrified to find June playing with some of these coins when she was a little girl of seven, and he had put them right back into the case while explaining to her that (a) these were not toys, and (b) her parents had gotten the money to start their very successful stationery company from their collection of rare American coins.

June stared down at the collection. "Why didn't you give me the key?" she moaned as if her parents could still hear her.

Only Mr. Mendax could unlock the case with a special key that he always carried with him, and that key was probably with The Authorities by now!

June tore her eyes away from the coins inside. She was there for a small, pale blue envelope leaning on top of the case. It had her initials, "J.S.," written on the front in her mother's loopy cursive. It always made her feel funny to see her mother's handwriting. She knew her parents best from photographs, and their handwriting made them seem closer and more real. June already knew what was inside the envelope. Shirley Rosenbloom had told June that her mother placed this envelope holding twelve pennies on top of the coin case on her very first birthday, and June received one birthday penny every year. Each penny came inside a clear plastic coin protector that snapped over the penny like a tiny, flat box, and June kept all her birthday pennies in a small silver dish shaped like a scallop shell. June loved her birthday tradition, but a few years ago she couldn't help but ask Shirley Rosenbloom why her mother gave her a penny every year, instead of one of the gold coins that looked like it was from a dragon's lair.

Shirley told her that now that her parents were gone, these were "pennies from heaven"; and every time you found a penny, it was a message from somebody who loved you in heaven. Even then, June knew that she was too old for that answer, but she always thought of her parents when she found a penny on the street. She figured that there must be another reason, and it must be a very important one, for her mother to set twelve pennies aside when she was only a baby. Each penny was numbered on the outside of the case, and for the hundredth time June wished that her mom had left a note telling her why she always gave her a special penny. But her mother had never expected that she wouldn't be there for every birthday, or that on the day she turned twelve, June would be handed a one-way ticket to South Dakota.

Indigo nudged her her ankle.

"Okay, okay, Indigo, I'm coming."

This was the last penny in the envelope. Maybe her mother had thought that after turning twelve June might want other, more grown-up presents. June held the small blue envelope in her hands and closed her eyes.

"Pennies from heaven," she whispered to herself, and opened the flap for the last time. Sure enough, there was the final penny in its little plastic case with the number twelve written on the corner in Magic Marker. June looked automatically at the year of the penny showing through the clear plastic window: 1965. Not an incredibly old coin, so it probably wasn't very valuable. Her mother and father had always been collectors, and some of the coins they saved were ones that they thought might become more valuable in time.

June stared at the gold coins locked safely inside the case, trying not to feel disappointed. Should she break it open? Smash the glass? Indigo growled warningly at her.

"You're right." She sighed. "I don't want to end up in jail like Mr. Mendax."

Indigo tugged hard on the lace of her ballet flat, with a glance toward the open door to the library. Now June could hear police sirens, and suddenly there was a loud pounding at the front door.

"Open up! Police!"

Indigo squealed and leaped into her arms. June pulled the secret door shut, quickly replacing the copy of *Alice in Wonderland* before she ran for the back door, which led out of the kitchen. She heard the front door opening and the thud of heavy feet. She slammed the kitchen door and ran down the stairs.

As soon as they got to the front entrance, Antonio blew twice on his silver whistle and waved his hand in the air as if there were no taxis left in all of

New York City. A bright yellow cab pulled up, and Antonio practically pushed June and Indigo into the backseat. "Take her to the airport!" Antonio said to the driver. He started to close the door, but June held on to the silver buttons of his uniform, wishing that her arms could reach all the way around his wide stomach. Antonio looked right into June's eyes, which were suddenly very blurry. Indigo whined and gently licked a tear she couldn't keep back. Antonio touched a hand to his heart. "I will pray for you," he said.

June stared at him as the taxi pulled away from the building. Then she looked up at Yoko Ono's living room and thought she saw a figure there—a petite woman with black hair and large sunglasses, dressed all in white. June Sparrow didn't exactly know Yoko, but they were neighbors and June worshipped her from afar. John Lennon and Yoko Ono—it was one of the greatest love stories of the twentieth century, and so much of it took place right there in the Dakota (even the horrible part). Growing up in the building, June had thought a lot about how strong and brave Yoko must be. She may look small but she is mighty, June explained to Indigo, who knew exactly what that was like.

June leaned her head out the back window, taking big gulps of air to steady her breathing. Looking up, she thought she saw Yoko brush her index finger against the side of her nose like Santa Claus. But Yoko would never do that, would she?

3
Another Dakota

Broke. Flat broke. This was going to take some getting used to, June thought as she looked out the airplane window. Indigo Bunting stirred impatiently inside the purse on her lap. It had taken the rest of her cash to pay for the taxi to the airport and the fee for Indigo to travel as a carry-on pet. The journey from Gray's Papaya to her seat on this airplane still seemed like a slow-moving dream to her—one of those nightmares that are so real, you force yourself back up to the surface to find yourself home in bed and safe as toast. Unfortunately, June Sparrow was wide awake.

The plane had flown through the night, and now it began its descent as the sun rose over the patchwork of fields below them. If she purposely blurred her vision, the landscape simplified into colored geometry. June pulled her tired eyes away from the window and took out the ziplock bag that Mr. Mendax had given her. Maybe there was a forgotten credit card in there, maybe she could check into a hotel when she got to South Dakota! She and Indigo Bunting could share a nice hot bubble bath, order room service, and the next day hop on a plane back to New York!

But Mr. Mendax was right: no cash, no credit card—these were the contents of her mother's wallet: an old South Dakota driver's license with a picture of her mom squinting at the camera, some gym membership cards that expired years ago, and a folded piece of paper that looked like it was ripped out of a spiral notebook. June unfolded the paper carefully, and inside was a wallet-size photo of her mother holding June as a baby. June suddenly realized that this might be the only picture she would ever have of herself and her mom, and she wished her dad was in it too—but he was probably behind the camera, so he was there too, in a way. She rubbed her finger gently over the image to wipe away any dust. Then she saw that something was written on the piece of paper in her mom's familiar handwriting.

At first she thought it was a shopping list, but what a strange list! At the top was what looked like a series of numbers and initials:

J.S. 2 R.B. 4 B.D.
Travel inside a beehive
Climb a ladder to the top of the world
Hug my oldest friend
Eat ice cream for breakfast
Take a ride on the La-Z-Boy express
Find metal that won't stick to a magnet
Let gonebyes go bye-bye

June read it over twice, then read it aloud to Indigo.

"What do you think it is?" she asked him. Since her parents had died nine years ago, this paper was at least that old. "They must have found the wallet on her bureau at the hotel or something, after the accident. A list of things she wanted to do?" June stared at the paper in her hand. "Anyone can eat ice cream for breakfast, I guess, especially if they're a grown-up—but travel inside a beehive?"

Indigo started snuffling hard at the top line with the initials.

"What is it, Indigo?"

Indigo rubbed his snout under the first two letters, then pushed his nose into her stomach. "J.S. 2 R.B. 4 B.D.?" June asked.

Indigo nodded vigorously, then shoved his nose hard into her stomach again.

June looked at the paper again.

"J.S.? J.S.! Wait! That's me! June Sparrow! Oh, Indigo, you really *are* a genius!"

Indigo gave her a smug look. He was better than June at riddles, and he was a master of the *New York Times* crossword puzzle, though June nearly always beat him at Scrabble.

"But what about the rest of it? '2 R.B. 4 B.D.' What does that mean?"

Indigo looked hard at the paper for several minutes, then gave a deep sigh.

"We'll figure it out," June said. "J.S. is me, it's always been me. She even wrote it on my birthday envelope. So one thing is for certain: this list has something to do with me."

The plane bumped onto the runway, and the force of the brakes pushed June hard against the back of her seat. Indigo scurried back inside the purse on her lap and she held tightly to it as the plane began to slow down. She suddenly whispered, "I love you, Indigo." Indigo nudged her with his nose through the side of the purse, and June took a deep breath as the plane taxied toward the gate.

June Sparrow was terrified.

June had always been able to find a way to make

things work out the way she thought they should. She had been incredibly bored by preschool. (The endless singing! The forced companionship! The ruthless diet of organic apple juice and sugar-free graham crackers!) So when it came time to apply to kindergarten, when most of the children who came from wealthy families were being brushed and drilled and even forced to wear something approximating a private-school uniform, June and Shirley Rosenbloom decided it was time for *homeschooling*.

Shirley and June hired a tutor for kindergarten, and June had plenty of play dates, but she could sleep as late as she wanted in the morning. Her parents' will left everything to her, and while Mr. Mendax was the designated trustee of her fortune, the will did not specifically state that he was empowered to make all decisions concerning June. June was an extremely articulate child, and Mr. Mendax was an extremely nervous person, even in the best of times. As long as Shirley Rosenbloom agreed, he thought it was fine for June to be privately tutored indefinitely. What Mr. Mendax didn't know was that for the last year June had decided to tutor herself. She gave the tutor a rather large check and told him that Shirley Rosenbloom was going to be taking over her lessons now that she was in middle school. Mr. Mendax was none the wiser.

Shirley was June's primary source of information about her parents, since she had been June's nanny before graduating to babysitter and eventually housekeeper, now that June didn't really need a babysitter anymore. June loved Shirley, and June was able to keep Shirley happy by eating well and never coming home late from one of her self-imposed field trips. June inhaled books and was extremely organized, so she always took her daily exercise in Central Park before settling down to read or study. She loved math, English, history, and science (after all, she got to choose what to study). In fact, the only thing that held zero interest for her was cooking, and Shirley Rosenbloom felt the same way: "I love you, darling, but I am too old to cook!" Shirley declared around the same time that June said goodbye to her tutor. So they ordered out for dinner (there were Chinese, Thai, Ethiopian, Indian, and Italian restaurants all within a few blocks). Shirley had whatever snacks June might be in the mood for during the day delivered by the grocery store where they had an account.

June was never lonely, because when she began to look into the best way to homeschool herself, she read that forming close friendships was an important part of the school experience. That very same day she saw a picture of a miniature pig online, and once she found out what neat and companionable pets they were, she sent off for the very best one she could find. Indigo Bunting arrived special delivery in his own crate filled with sweet grass and cotton wool. She hadn't been lonely since the day he arrived, and she never quite understood what it meant to be bored when you had an apple in your pocket and a great city to wander.

But now all that was over.

"Welcome to Sioux Falls, South Dakota!" read the banner opposite the gate as June walked off the plane. She looked around expectantly, but there was nobody there to meet her. Did her aunt even know she was coming? Her heart sank. She went into the ladies' room, and once she was inside a stall, she took Indigo Bunting out of his bag. He had slept on his velvet cape and was wearing his top hat—which was a little crushed but still gave him a jaunty air.

June held him to her chest and gulped hard; now that nobody could see her, she couldn't manage to be brave anymore. Indigo snuffled her cheek, she kissed his perfect pink snout, and after a few minutes she managed to blow her nose. She held Indigo up so that he looked her right in the eye, and he gave her an encouraging nod.

"You're right, Indigo. This is a temporary setback, that's all. We'll find our way back to the real Dakota no matter what." Her voice trembled, and Indigo licked her cheek again. "I know," she said, snuggling him close to her chest. "The main thing is . . . we're together."

4
Not in Kansas Anymore

June didn't see any sign of a taxi stand, which seemed a little strange, but even stranger was the fact that there was nobody else in the terminal. Before she went into the bathroom, there had been a few people waiting for their baggage and talking on their cell phones. She hadn't been gone that long, but now this entire airport, which was really just one big room, was totally deserted. The empty baggage carousel was still going around, and even though June didn't have anything to collect, she walked right up to the opening where the baggage disappeared behind dirty rubber flaps and yelled, "Hello! Anybody there?"

No answer. She looked out the front door. Nobody. She looked through the windows at the tarmac. There were three fat planes painted solid gray that looked like cartoon drawings of the United States Air Force, but not a soldier in sight.

Indigo wriggled in her arms and looked up at her with a cocked eyebrow.

"What is it, Indigo?"

She set him down, and he trotted over to the door facing the parking lot and scratched expectantly.

"Okay, okay." She walked over to let him out, figuring he needed to use the facilities. But once she opened the door, he ran around behind her and nudged her legs forward. "Fine! I guess we're going outside," she said. "Not that there's anything out there."

But as soon as she got through the doors, she stopped. Right there in front of her was this *gi-nor-mous* sky! There were no tall buildings, just rows of trees placed like toys on the landscape, and the sky took up most of the space for your eyes.

"Holy Saskatchewan Sunday, Indigo!" Then she felt the wind. It might have been unseasonably warm in New York City the night she left, but here in South Dakota there was a cold wind whipping across the farmlands without any buildings to break its impact on her bare legs. It turned out that a silk dress with pink tulle was not highly functional outerwear in the South Dakota prairie.

June stamped her feet in the cold, hoping that would make a difference, but it didn't. Indigo was shivering, and she picked him up to give him a hug. Where were all the people? Where were all the cabs? There wasn't even a vehicle in sight.

No, that wasn't true. There was one small silver rectangle moving slowly along the highway in the direction of the airport. Great, one car, June thought, and I don't even know if it's coming to the airport or on its way somewhere else. She went back inside the terminal so that she and Indigo wouldn't catch colds that turned into pneumonia and hastened them to an early grave, just like Mimi in *La Bohème*. It was all Mr. Mendax's fault. Some guardian! It was ridiculous that she had been packed off to South Dakota without even a phone number to call her mythical aunt Bridget.

She walked back and forth, wishing she had her cell phone or a book. For once she had none of the above since she had only been going to the opera, and the purse she'd brought with her had exactly enough room for Indigo Bunting, cash, and a house key. Now the cash was gone and the house key was useless.

The doors to the terminal slid open with a loud swoosh to reveal a bulky figure with a stern expression on her face. Even though June had never met her in person before, there was no doubt about it: Aunt Bridget had arrived.

She was wearing serious rubber boots, nothing like the fashionable rain boots that women wore in New York. These boots were army-issue green, and the brown over the toes was not a design element; it was mud. Aunt Bridget stood in the doorway, hands on hips. As a matter of fact, she stood directly in the doorway, so that the automatic doors kept trying to close and, finding her immovable, bounced back. She had short brown hair with some streaks of gray, and the kind of face middle-aged people get when they've spent most of their lives outdoors. June stared and Aunt Bridget stared. Then June remembered her manners and held out her hand.

"Aunt Bridget?"

"You're June." A statement, not a question. Her aunt still didn't move forward, though June had taken a few steps toward her. June let her hand drift down. Apparently a handshake was not going to take place, never mind a hug. "Any luggage?"

"No." June was usually a motormouth, but she couldn't quite make small talk at the moment. The woman in front of her looked about as much like a farmer as June could imagine. Aunt Bridget was wearing overalls, a checked shirt, a John Deere cap, and one of those heavy men's coats that look preppy

when clean, but when serving their original pur-
pose as a farm jacket most likely never get cleaned
at all.

"Come on then," Aunt Bridget said, and she
turned and walked out. June picked up Indigo from
where he had been hiding behind her legs and followed Aunt Bridget out the door. A silver Cadillac
Seville was parked at the curb—the shining rectangle she had seen in the distance. June stared at
the car, then back at Aunt Bridget, who was already
opening the driver's side door. This couldn't really
be her car! But Aunt Bridget got into the driver's
seat, and June suddenly thought that her aunt might
just leave without her. June hurried around to the
passenger side and scooted in, placing Indigo on her
lap. He put his ears back and tried to become even
smaller than he already was. Aunt Bridget wrinkled
her nose.

"What's that?" she asked, her hand on the ignition key. Everything in the car was perfect, and the
scent of pine drifted from a tree-shaped air fresh-
ener hanging from the rearview mirror.

"This is Indigo," June said, holding him up under his armpits, trying to be charming. Indigo smiled, though June could feel his little body trembling. "He's my best friend."

Aunt Bridget looked long and hard at Indigo. "That's a pig," she said finally, as if this needed to be confirmed before she drove anywhere.

"He's a miniature pig," June said, accustomed to this response. "They are the cleanest pet you can own."

"Hmmph!" Aunt Bridget turned the key, and the engine started with a deep humming sound. "Pigs can be clean if they're kept right." This sounded hopeful, if noncommittal. June looked at her aunt's muddy boots on the perfect black carpet of the car and wondered how she kept it so nice. "He doesn't smell too bad. But in the future: no livestock in the car."

"Indigo's not livestock!" June said, horrified. "He's like—like—a cat or a dog!"

Aunt Bridget eyed Indigo coldly. He curled into a ball in June's lap, trying to become invisible.

"Dogs and cats live outside on the farm," Aunt Bridget said. "Sleep in the barn."

"The barn!" June stared at her and held Indigo up next to her heart. "Indigo always sleeps with me! And he doesn't smell. He never smells! He's cleaner than I am." June realized that this might not be the best thing to say. She tried another tactic: "If he sleeps in the barn, I'll sleep in the barn too!"

Aunt Bridget shrugged and pulled out of the parking lot. "I've got some clothes you can borrow so you don't catch your death," she said without taking her eyes off the road.

They both stared out of the windshield without speaking for what felt like a very long time. June almost spoke twice, but stopped, afraid her voice would come out with a quaver. She didn't want to quaver, not here, not now.

June finally spoke again: "Nice car."

Aunt Bridget's mouth softened just a little. "It was my father's," she said. Then, a moment later, she added, "Your grandfather's. He and your grandmother died within a year of each other when I was fifteen. Roseanne was fourteen."

"So you're an orphan, too!" June said. "You and my mom, I mean."

Aunt Bridget nodded without taking her eyes off the road. She pressed down harder on the gas pedal, even though the Cadillac was already going over eighty miles an hour.

June thought of about fifty things to say, but instead she checked that her seat belt was fastened and looked out the side window. Tall rows of cornstalks whipped by like miniature forests with pathways running through in absolutely straight lines. The heat was on and her bare feet were finally warming up inside her ballet flats.

"It is a very nice car," June said again, proud that there was no quaver at all. None on the outside, anyway.

5
The Farm

"Get out of the way, you darn cluckers!" growled Aunt Bridget. She pulled into a long dirt driveway, and several chickens fluttered out of the way. "Talk about dumb!" Aunt Bridget steered the Cadillac expertly around potholes filled with rainwater, and June gripped Indigo so tightly, he had to squeak to tell her to loosen her grip. Aunt Bridget's highway speed had hovered right around ninety miles per hour; out here there was nothing to slow her down.

The driveway led up a hill to a farmhouse with a pickup truck parked in front of a high red barn. Aunt Bridget stopped the Cadillac with a jolt in front of the small back porch. "This is it," she said, and she was out of the car before June caught her breath from the sudden stop.

June opened the passenger door and tried to step gingerly onto the muddy ground. It did no good—her ballet flats immediately filled with cold, dirty sludge. She couldn't help a small shriek. She turned to see Aunt Bridget surveying her from top to bottom.

"I didn't have time to change," June began. "I was at the opera, and Mr. Mendax—"

"Mr. Mendax! Hmmph!" Aunt Bridget gave that expressive snort again. "A man who cries over money is no kind of man. Spilt milk."

Well, at least there's something we can agree on, thought June.

"I'm going out to the barn." Aunt Bridget jerked her thumb toward the house without moving from the driveway. "You can use your mother's old room.

Might be some clothes up there. Extra boots on the porch." She stomped off toward the barn.

June slogged up the front steps and wondered if her flats would ever come back to life. The back porch was strewn with rubber boots facing different directions as if they had been dropped like jacks from a giant hand. Not one pair looked like it would fit her, and just when she thought she couldn't cry any more, she couldn't stop. She stood on that tiny porch and sobbed aloud: big gulping sobs that got louder the harder she tried to stifle them. Indigo whined desperately as he tried to lick every tear, but this time there were too many. She wished Aunt Bridget had taken a moment to let her into the house; now she felt like even more of a stranger. Indigo wriggled down from her arms and pushed the door open with his nose. He ran back and put his front legs on her calves, staring up with a pleading look.

"I know, I know," June managed, picking him up again. "I'm just cold and tired, Indigo, that's all."

She took a deep breath, and with one kiss between Indigo's ears for courage she walked into the house. A light switch illuminated a rose-colored globe in the ceiling, and the soft light was encouraging. She slipped out of her shoes so that she wouldn't track dirt and continued barefoot down a hallway on braided rugs placed like stepping stones over the cold wooden floor. She passed a dining room that looked as if nobody had eaten there in a very long time, and entered the large kitchen.

It smelled of apples and cinnamon. There was a case of Mason jars on the counter and a wire contraption hanging in the middle of the room with tiers of drying apple slices swaying in the invisible breath of the house. This is what makes everything smell so good in here, June thought as she looked more closely.

June's heart lifted for the first time, and she moved closer to what she thought must be a fruit dryer. How long would it take to core, peel, and slice so many apples? Wasn't this kind of thing cheaper to buy? She delicately lifted one slice, afraid the whole thing would come unbalanced, but in fact it seemed sturdy enough. She didn't particularly like dried apples, but she had eaten only a small bag of mini pretzels on the plane and she was starving.

At first bite her mouth flooded with an ecstatic lemony cinnamon flavor that had nothing to do with those rubbery white things she sometimes found inside an otherwise crunchy and delicious bag of trail mix. Indigo murmured his contentment as she gave him the next slice, then reached for one more, well, maybe two more . . . it already felt like an awfully long day.

June managed to stop herself from eating a whole layer of apples, mostly out of fear of Aunt Bridget. She did help herself to some milk from an actual glass bottle in the refrigerator (the most modern appliance in the kitchen) and grabbed a corn muffin from a Tupperware container on the counter. Indigo's nose led them to an earthenware jar containing the best gingersnaps she had ever tasted, with crystallized sugar on top. There were plenty, so June tried stacking up apple slices with a gingersnap on each side like a gingersnap-apple Oreo. Indigo approved. After another glass of milk, four buttered corn muffins and three cookie sandwiches, June and Indigo had finally taken the edge off, and she felt more like herself again—herself in a very strange dream, maybe, but still June Sparrow.

She leaned back in her chair and placed Indigo on her lap as they took in the place. Hanging on the wall over the kitchen sink was a small decorative plate with a painted pig and chicken. There were white curtains in the windows and a potted geranium on the sill, but this was clearly a working kitchen, not the kind of place where you lingered over coffee and the *New York Times* crossword puzzle. June and Indigo's favorite weekends started with the crossword and ended with a nice long Scrabble tournament before bed. She wondered if her aunt even owned a Scrabble board.

"Not a lot of lingering around here, I'll bet," June said to Indigo. "I wonder where the dishwasher is." Not only was there no dishwasher, but there were no sponges—just a thin cloth rag draped over the clean dishes in the drainer. June brought the rag gingerly to her nose before using it. Not exactly pleasant, but June went ahead and used the same cloth to wash her glass and wipe up any crumbs that she and Indigo might have left behind. Aunt Bridget sure could cook, but that didn't make her any less scary.

June was glad there was hot water coming out of the tap, and that she wasn't going to have to heat water on the stove like in *Little House on the Prairie*. She couldn't remember the last time she washed a dish by hand, and it wasn't exactly warm in the house, though certainly better than outside. "Guess I'd better find us some clothes," she said, thinking of her cozy shearling coat hanging in the closet in the Dakota. It was probably sold already! And what had happened to Shirley Rosenbloom? She would have to go live with her son, Harold, in Long Island City, and Mr. Mendax might be in prison for life. June sighed deeply, but Indigo wriggled off her lap and led the way out of the kitchen. June followed, grateful that they were on their own for a bit longer. Maybe, if she was lucky, she wouldn't see Aunt Bridget until dinnertime.

Then she saw the hardware-store calendar by the door and stopped: every square was filled with tiny handwriting. June took a closer look. Each day was like a diary, a list of everything Aunt Bridget had done that day, crossed off neatly: "Go to feed store, Refill bird feeders, Pay bills, Take pullets to 4H Club," and on and on. Did she fill this out before bed every night?

"I hope she doesn't make me fill out a calendar," June muttered, then quickly looked at today's date. "Pick up niece/airport, Pick up feed for chickens, Recycle milk bottles."

"Huh," said June. "Niece! Nice. I don't even get a name."

Indigo had been circling impatiently, and now he pushed the backs of June's ankles, nudging her toward the stairs. "Okay, okay!" she said.

Marching up the wall next to the stairway were framed family photos, and she looked long and hard at each one, looking for her mother, but most of them were photos of her grandparents. Here they were at the farm, here they were in front of the Cadillac, here they were as young parents holding a baby, but how could June tell which baby? Bridget was older and Roseanne was younger; that was about all June knew. Then she saw the one color photo: it was Bridget and her mother as teenagers, leaning their heads together. They were both wearing bathing suits and had their arms around each other's shoulders, smiling at the camera with nineties hairstyles: Bridget was a layered blonde and Roseanne was a spiky redhead.

June didn't even know her grandparents' names. Shirley Rosenbloom had told her that her grandparents on both sides died before she was born. June wasn't sure what she really felt looking at these old photos on the stairs. These grandparents looked friendly enough, but how could you miss something you never had in the first place? June looked again at the photo of teenaged Aunt Bridget and her mother, wondering if their own parents were still alive when they took this picture. June never would have recognized Aunt Bridget from the happy girl in this picture.

"Come on, Indigo," June said a little harshly, though she had been the one stopping at every picture. Indigo gave her a hurt look and stalked up the rest of the stairs. (He could be a little oversensitive sometimes—it was his artistic temperament.) There was a small landing at the top and three closed doors. June sighed. How was she supposed to know which room was her mother's? But Indigo had no doubt which way to go. He led her to the door on the left and scratched, looking over his shoulder to be sure she was paying attention.

June turned the glass doorknob and stepped inside. "Indigo!" she gasped. "How did you know?" The room was painted pink, but not a repellant baby pink, a truly fabulous pink that seemed to have some kind of extra shine to it. There were movie posters from the eighties and nineties on the walls. One whole wall was covered with actual LPs nailed to the wall, with hundreds of pennies glued around them in bright copper rays and curlicues. June stood in the center of the room, trying to take it all in. This was the most color she had seen since she got off the plane! This was her mom's bedroom—she knew without asking.

It was exactly how she would have done her own room if she had lived in those days, but to actually glue things directly on the walls! June had never thought of that. Then there was the bed. It wasn't just a bed, but a canopy bed. There were white curtains above and around the bed, an Indian-print bedspread, and some throw pillows with silk screens of movie stars on the covers: James Dean and Audrey Hepburn. There was even a small desk with a gooseneck lamp. And then June's heart leaped: a *turntable*!

It was one of those old suitcase-style turntables in the absolute perfect color: light blue. There were records stacked next to it and an actual beanbag chair on the floor within easy reach of the music. Her mom might have been born in the eighties, but she had definitely been into vintage stuff. June opened the suitcase, and there was a record still on the turntable: the sound track to *Grease*! It couldn't get any better than this, unless . . . June found the volume knob and turned it on so that the little red light glowed. She held her breath as she gently put the needle down on the record, and "Summer Nights" pounded out of the speakers.

June screamed aloud and immediately started dancing in the middle of the room. Indigo joined her, bumping his hip against her ankle. They had both watched the movie more times than they could count, and they used to take turns being John Travolta and Olivia Newton-John, though Indigo always wanted to be Travolta.

"Thought I told you the pig wasn't allowed inside." Aunt Bridget's voice broke through the music, and June and Indigo both froze. In Indigo's case this meant he toppled onto his side, a very undignified position, though he quickly recovered himself and scurried behind June's legs. Aunt Bridget walked into the room and lifted the needle from the record. The silence was stunning. June stood and stared. Aunt Bridget turned back toward her and the silence lengthened. No wonder she lives alone, thought June. She's just plain mean.

"So you found Roseanne's room," Aunt Bridget said dryly. "And her records."

June nodded.

"Find something to eat?"

June nodded.

"Supper's at six. I'll expect help with that."

June nodded again. Aunt Bridget eyed Indigo. "How much does the pig weigh?"

"Four pounds, three ounces."

"As big as he gets?"

"He's full grown," June said hesitantly. She wasn't sure what her aunt was really asking.

"Not much bacon."

June's eyes widened, then narrowed. "*No* bacon," she said, and this time she didn't even try to hide her rage. "*No* bacon. *No* sausage. Indigo is my friend. Where he goes, I go."

Aunt Bridget seemed unimpressed. "He won't be going to school with you in the morning." She shrugged. "But he can spend the day in the barn with the others."

"School?!" June shrieked. "I don't go to school."

"No?" Aunt Bridget raised an eyebrow. "Maybe that explains it."

"Explains what?"

"You go to school here in South Dakota," she said, ignoring June's question. "Bus comes at six forty a.m. Against the law not to attend school here, got it?"

"Maybe." June was steely eyed.

"Well, you're getting on that bus in the morning, and the critter is sleeping in the barn."

"Then I'm sleeping in the barn!"

Aunt Bridget looked out the window. "Nights not too cold, yet." And she turned and left the room just like that.

June closed the door without slamming it even though she was tempted, grabbed Indigo, and fell onto her mother's bed. Indigo wedged himself as close to her as he could. "I hate her," she whispered to Indigo. "Hate, hate, hate!" Indigo snuffled back with just the right balance of sympathy and indignation. June grabbed her purse and started to rifle through it. Her entire fortune amounted to $4.65, not including her birthday penny, which she was never going to spend. She pulled out her mother's list again. Maybe if she could figure out the list, she could figure out a way to get the money to go home.

She read it out loud to Indigo:

"J.S. 2 R.B. 4 B.D.
Travel inside a beehive
Climb a ladder to the top of the world
Hug my oldest friend
Eat ice cream for breakfast
Take a ride on the La-Z-Boy express
Find metal that won't stick to a magnet
Let gonebyes go bye-bye"

Suddenly there was the sound of a gunshot, then another one, LOUD! June jumped up to look out the window, and there was Aunt Bridget with a rifle on her shoulder, sighting the bird feeder. The bushy tail of a gray squirrel whipped up the tree, and the rifle report came again. This time June saw wood flying off the bark where the bullet hit home.

"She's crazy," breathed June. "It's safer in New York City! Come on, Indigo. We're better off in the barn."

Indigo shook his head thoughtfully as June carefully folded the list and put it into her pocket. Her old life inside the real Dakota had never seemed so far away. How would she ever get home?

June opened her mother's closet. There were mostly summer dresses, but here and there was a flannel shirt, and against the back wall was a small white dresser with a drawer full of blue jeans. They were big on her, but she found a belt and rolled them up. She pulled a dress off a hanger and buttoned a flannel shirt over the top, knowing she would still be cold, but at least it was a little bit fashionable. She grabbed a lumpy green scarf and matching hat that looked hand knit from the top drawer.

June stopped—woven in between the stitches was a tiny glint of red. She touched it gently. It wasn't a thread, it was one strand of hair. Her mother's long red hair, which June wished she had inherited along with her green eyes. June had gotten her father's dark brown hair and brown eyes, which she thought were terribly boring, though Indigo had brown eyes as well, and he was quite vain about them (she had caught him blinking his long lashes in the mirror more than once). Everything looked better on a miniature pig. June sighed. She held the scarf up to her nose and smelled something she just barely recognized: the scent of her mother. She stayed there for a moment, thinking hard, then wrapped the scarf tightly around her neck, picked up Indigo, and closed the door behind her. How could she miss what she could hardly remember?

6
Barnyard Blues

It was cold. Wretchedly cold. Plus it smelled. June couldn't honestly decide if she liked the smell or not. It was that dense, loamy scent of farm animals that was equal parts nice and nasty. June tried to get comfortable on the floor of the tack room, where Aunt Bridget had told her she would find a pile of horse blankets. Blankets were an overstatement, in June's opinion. These were filthy, quilted things that had clearly been worn many times by large animals in bad weather. June unfolded one to put underneath her and Indigo and pulled the other one on top. But it didn't work. Nothing worked. Plus June's stomach was growling because she was too proud to go back into the house for dinner after she and Indigo made a dramatic exit to the barn.

She pulled her mother's knit hat farther down so that it covered her eyes and pulled Indigo even closer. He was hungry too, though he wasn't complaining—in fact, he was being uncharacteristically compliant. June wondered if it was a bit intimidating for him to be surrounded by all these animals, since he had never been in a barn before. Now that it was well and truly dark outside, June had to admit that whatever hope she had that Aunt Bridget would worry about them looked to be a complete waste of time. In the books, your long-lost aunt would come out to the barn with a warm plate of food. Apparently Aunt Bridget hadn't read the right books.

June had grabbed a Nancy Drew mystery from her mother's bookshelf as she left the bedroom, and she liked Nancy Drew well enough, but when she tried reading aloud to Indigo, he yawned loudly and closed his eyes. "Okay, forget it!" June said, slamming the book shut. "Since it's too cold to sleep, let's see who's here."

Indigo looked up at her in alarm. Sometimes June got a little reckless when she was frustrated, and Indigo knew that tone of voice. June threw off the top blanket and swept him up in her arms. They walked out of the tack room and stopped at the first stall they came to. A brown cow with a small white blaze on her chest lifted her head and blinked at them, her long lashes seeming to take forever to rise and fall. June reached out her hand, and as she touched that soft, inviting nose, she felt some of her anger start to ease.

"I know it's a little late to visit," June said. "But we're new here. I'm June and this is Indigo." The cow blinked slowly again, and June held Indigo out so that he could exchange sniffs with her. The cow sniffed once, twice, and raised her eyebrows in surprise. "Yes, he's a pig," said June. "You could say he's . . . the runt of the litter."

Indigo gave her a dirty look, but June pressed on. "He's a little sensitive about his size, but in terms of miniature pigs, he is a fine example of the breed."

"Sorry, Indigo," she whispered into his ear. "I don't want to overwhelm them."

Indigo wriggled out of her arms and jumped to the floor of the barn, which was hard dirt. June was worried he might hurt himself jumping so far, but Indigo shook himself briefly and marched right down the center aisle. June could swear the cow was smiling. "He can be a little stubborn," she said apologetically. "Typical New Yorker." The cow smiled even more, then pulled a bit of hay out of the rack in front of her and chewed steadily. June's stomach growled.

Indigo was scratching impatiently at the next stall, and June lifted him up to stare at the wide, brown rump of a horse. Indigo rested his trotters on the top of the stall door and sniffed as loudly as he could, but the horse only shifted his weight from one back hoof to another.

"Hello?" June tried tentatively, wishing that

she had a carrot or an apple or a lump of sugar like the girls in books always did, but she didn't have a thing. The horse continued to ignore them. There was a nameplate on the stall: "Mr. Chips." June tried again. "Mr. Chips?" At this the horse stamped hard and flicked his ears but kept his rear end facing directly toward them. Then the tail lifted and the horse deposited some manure right there in front of them! June pulled Indigo back quickly and took a few steps away in shock.

"How rude!" she said out loud, and thought she could almost hear laughter coming from the horse stall. "Well, you don't have to poop *and* laugh in our faces!" she said indignantly. The laughter got even louder, and June realized it was not coming from the horse, which had lowered his tail and still not turned to look at them (rude thing). There was someone else in there. Tiptoeing back, June and Indigo peered over the edge of the stall, and there was a small, round-bellied goat staring up at them. He must have been hiding behind the horse, but now he stood right up on his hind legs and rested his front hooves on the stall door to survey them.

He had a sly look, though that could have been due to the horns and silky goatee, which did not exactly inspire confidence. He was snorting and wheezing, most definitely laughing at them. June gathered as much self-possession as she could and held out her hand.

"My name is June Sparrow," she said. The goat allowed her to shake his hoof, though his eyes narrowed to slits so that he appeared to be even more amused. "And this is Indigo Bunting. We've just arrived here from New York."

At this the goat gave them both an appraising look. He sniffed at Indigo, who kept his trotters to himself and extended his snub nose as warily as if he was being introduced to a leopard that everyone assured you had been raised as a house cat.

"A pleasure," said June briskly, and with one more glance at the horse's backside, she continued down the line of stalls with Indigo poking his head out from beneath her arm. The goat stared at them, leaning his head to the side so that he could rub his little black horns on the wall.

"Tough customer," June whispered to Indigo.

The next few stalls were empty, but when they reached the last one, Indigo began to sniff with a great deal of interest. Inside was a fresh bed of hay and a low trough filled with what could only be described as compost. June opened the door warily, but the stall was empty. She plopped down on the hay and let go of Indigo, who moved quickly to the trough and clambered inside. He ducked his head down and stood there eating the stuff.

"Indigo Bunting!" June was shocked. "You are standing in garbage and eating it!"

Indigo gave her a deeply apologetic look but kept right on eating.

June sighed and lay back in the hay, which actually smelled good and was quite a bit warmer than a horse blanket if you burrowed in a bit. Of course she had read *Charlotte's Web*, but so far she had met no spiders in the barn, and she had a bad feeling. Clearly, this was a pigpen. Clearly, Aunt Bridget had put the hay and slops out here, figuring that

Indigo would end up right here doing exactly this. June propped herself up on her elbows and watched Indigo eat. He was a very tidy eater, but he was willing to stand in a pig trough rather than miss a meal if given the chance. This was not a good sign. Then she looked on the wall at the back of the barn just past the pigpen. Her heart skipped a beat, and she had to put a hand over her mouth to keep silent.

Hanging on a nail on the wall was a heavy butcher knife. On the floor below was a broad tree stump that had to be as old as the barn itself, maybe even as old as Aunt Bridget. June got up quietly, so as not to alert Indigo, and peered more closely. By the bare bulb that lit this end of the barn, she could see that the top of the stump was deeply scored with marks of a blade. June looked even more closely. "Holy Saskatchewan Sunday," she breathed. In every score on the wood there were bloodstains. This wasn't an old tree stump; this was a chopping block.

7
First Day

The horror of the morning: woken by Aunt Bridget for a breakfast that had more meat and eggs than June had ever seen on one plate; the hay that stuck in her hair; the old toothbrush she had to use and the clothes from her mother's closet that didn't fit right. Aunt Bridget must have brought out a warm blanket at some point in the night, because June woke up with a brightly colored afghan tucked around her shoulders. That was a nice surprise, because the hardest part was the fact that it was still dark outside.

It was dark when Aunt Bridget shook her awake in the pigpen and dark when she pushed scrambled eggs around her plate; dark when the school bus stopped at the end of the driveway, where Aunt Bridget waited in the warm Cadillac with the motor running while June had to stand out in the cold "to make sure the driver sees you because you're new."

June had never ridden on a school bus before, but what she had seen in the movies scared her. Kids were always being beaten up or forced to eat the contents of other kids' lunch boxes while the driver behaved like a prison guard. When the long yellow bus pulled up, she saw a few faces pressed against the steamed-up windows and wondered which one of those kids would soon be shoving her off a playground swing.

She took a deep breath and pulled her mother's flannel-lined farm jacket closer around her. She had never been so cold, and she was separated from Indigo for the first time since they'd left New York.

She had tried to sneak him out under her jacket, but Aunt Bridget had looked at her with that X-ray vision and said, "If you want the pig impounded by Animal Control, you can take him to school. Otherwise, you can leave him in the barn."

June climbed the three high steps onto the bus, and the driver nodded at her with a businesslike smile, then waved past her at the Cadillac. June turned and saw the headlights pull back as Aunt Bridget put the car into reverse. She can't wait to leave, thought June. The bus was strangely quiet and June hesitated at the front. Every seat looked full and most of the kids were slumped against the windows. It was not yet seven in the morning. The driver pulled the doors shut with the big handle, and the bus hissed and groaned.

"Find yourself a seat," the driver said, and June realized that underneath the bulky jacket and wool cap was a woman, not a man. In the movies the driver was always a man, and the bus was filled with screaming children. June walked down the silent aisle, submitting to the judgment. She knew that most of the kids were only pretending to be asleep. There were several spots with only one kid on the wide black seats, but nobody moved over. June went all the way to the back, holding on to the tops of the seats as she went. Every step felt like she was on trial, but she kept her balance.

This was easier than the subway, where she used to stand in the middle of the car and pretend she was a surfer: no hands. Shirley Rosenbloom always worried when June took the subway instead of a taxi, but June happily took public transportation whenever it suited her. She had yet to see a bus or a taxi in South Dakota.

The very last seat had the faint smell of tuna fish, which June realized was coming from a boy slumped against the window like the rest. She stood for a moment, not knowing if she should walk all the way back down the line; then Tunafish Boy moved his feet over to make room, down below the seats where nobody else would see. June took this as a yes, and sat down. Tunafish Boy scooted over and didn't open his eyes. June stared straight ahead at the road in front of the bus, way down at the end of this long, long aisle. It was finally starting to get light outside. Rows of corn, rows of brown earth, and hay bales wrapped in white plastic were placed on this platter of land like candy for a giant. Nothing in sight was recognizable as the life of June Sparrow.

"June Sparrow?" The homeroom teacher's voice sounded harsh above the scraping of chairs and whispering voices.

"Present." June had seen kids in classrooms in movies and on TV, but so far nothing at this school looked like it did in the movies.

The teacher stopped and looked at her. "Present?" A few kids laughed, and June sat up straighter. She already knew that attending middle school was not the best way to get an education; that's why she homeschooled herself. But she still wanted to try to blend in with kid camouflage. She was pretending that she was a scientist gathering data for a research project on the habits of sixth graders in the mid-western region of the United States of America.

"Welcome to Red Bank Middle School," the homeroom teacher said with strenuous cheer. There were thumbtacks sticking through corrugated yellow borders around the blackboard and cloud-shaped cutouts taped along the edge of the ceiling with affirmations written inside: "Your Best Is Always Good Enough!" "Turn That Frown Upside Down!" "Be the Person You Want to Be!" The teacher was wearing a sweaterdress and chunky necklace over purple velour leggings and she seemed very determined to be a Bright Spot in Your Day. June thought it was a little early in the morning for this sort of thing, but she was taking notes on the dress and habits of local flora and fauna.

"Thank you," June said politely, but she wasn't sure if the teacher heard her, because the bell rang again. (There was a lot of bell ringing in school—she hadn't known about that.) Everyone scrambled to get to their first class, and June made her way to the front of the room.

"I'm Ms. Huff," the teacher said, smiling at June

as she handed her a piece of paper with a grid laid out on it—just like the South Dakota landscape. "Here's your schedule. English is first period. Better scoot!"

June didn't think she had ever heard anyone use the verb "scoot" before. She opened her mouth to say something, thought better of it, and gave Ms. Huff an upside-down frown. The hallway was packed with people banging lockers and pushing past each other—everything was loud and confusing—and then suddenly it was totally empty. June eased herself away from the wall, where she had pressed herself to avoid the crush, and began to wander down the hall looking for the classroom on her schedule. June had never been inside any school before, and she wished there were signs telling her where to go, or even a map with a big red dot saying, "You Are Here."

A teacher came hurrying past, and when June stopped him to ask directions he gave a quick, irritated look at her schedule, then pointed her up a wide set of stairs. His frown was *not* upside down.

June trudged up the main staircase, still carrying the army-style backpack she had found under her mother's bed. She didn't have a locker yet and worried that her bag would begin to smell as much as Tunafish Boy's. There was a ham and egg sandwich inside that Aunt Bridget had made for her with the assumption that lunch and breakfast only had to diverge in form, not content. She didn't seem to comprehend that June did not eat pork. June hadn't wanted to frighten Indigo when she saw the axe in the barn, but this morning she told him to be very careful to keep his distance from Aunt Bridget. New York might be the only place where people really understood pigs as pets. She had to get them back to the real Dakota as soon as possible.

June sighed and looked back at her schedule. There was a large window at the top of the stairs, and she saw some high school kids in the parking lot leaning against their cars. It looked just like *Grease* without the fun musical numbers. She wandered down the hall until she finally found the classroom with the number that matched her schedule.

A second bell had rung about five minutes ago, but everything looked the same in these hallways with their horizontal stripes of green paint over beige walls. June took a deep breath and opened the door as quietly as she could. The teacher wasn't sitting at his desk in front of the room—that seat was empty and a blond boy with skin almost as pale as his hair was standing at the front of the room. June wrinkled her nose—it was Tunafish Boy! He had been reading from a piece of paper but stopped and stared as June tried to edge inside. The teacher raised his thick eyebrows but didn't move his corduroy-jacket-clad self from the windowsill, where he was leaning back and listening to the report.

"Yes?" the teacher said.

"I'm sorry I'm late."

"Are you in the right room?"

"I think so," June said, checking her schedule again. "Mr. Fitzroy? English?"

The teacher nodded without saying anything.

"I'm June Sparrow," she said, slipping into an empty desk in the front row. "I'm new."

Mr. Fitzroy looked at her for a long moment. He had gray hair and his tie was thrown over his shoulder as if he had flipped it out of the way when he ate breakfast that morning. His wide-framed glasses made his eyes look far away, and it was impossible to tell what he was thinking.

"It's nearly the end of September," he said flatly.

"Yes, it is," June said, and was surprised when she heard some giggles and saw the teacher frown. She hadn't meant to be rude. She was failing badly at kid camouflage and thought of something she had heard somewhere, probably one of those nature shows she and Indigo liked to watch on TV. When it comes right down to it, there are only three laws of the universe for all living organisms: adapt, migrate, or die. Death was certainly the least complicated of the three options, and it looked like she was headed for sudden death this morning.

June pulled out a notebook and pen from her mother's backpack. The teacher turned back to Tunafish Boy and nodded for him to continue.

"Go ahead, Joe."

"*The Red Badge of Courage* is the book I liked most on my summer reading list," said Joe in a stronger voice than she would have expected from someone who hunched his shoulders as if he wanted to appear shorter than he really was. He read his book report straight through, and June thought it was pretty good. She wondered how many books they were required to read over the summer and why they were still going over the summer reading list at the end of September. At least they were talking about something she liked.

"June Sparrow," the teacher called out after Joe went back to his seat. June looked up, surprised. "Did you do any reading this summer that you would like to share with the class?"

June nodded. "I read lots of books this summer, but I haven't prepared—written anything about them. . . ." She let her sentence trail off. Why had she drawn attention to the fact that she was behind and ill prepared?

"A lot of books? Really? Why don't you come up and tell us about your favorite one." The teacher sounded a bit sarcastic and June looked at him sharply, wondering how she had managed to get on his bad side so quickly. But if there was one thing June Sparrow didn't like, it was having anyone doubt her word. Of *course* she had read a lot of books this summer. She wouldn't have said it otherwise! She stood up, taking her notebook with her. Even though there was nothing written inside, it made her feel less alone.

She turned to face the class, but it was hard to get started. The last row had kids with their heads down on the desk and their legs stretched far out in front. The front row was mostly girls who had their desks perfectly arranged with matching binders and notebooks. The middle of the classroom was harder to define, but right now everyone was staring at her. They didn't look unfriendly, but they didn't look exactly friendly either, just blank eyed. Mr. Fitzroy nodded for her to begin and crossed his arms. There were large leather elbow patches on his jacket.

"My favorite book this summer was *Pride and*

Prejudice, by Jane Austen," June began. "Actually, I haven't quite finished it yet—it's a pretty long book, but—"

"Haven't quite finished it?" the teacher interrupted. "But you know how it ends, don't you? Since you saw the movie?"

June was shocked. "I didn't see the movie," she said. "I want to—but I never see the movie before I've read the book."

"Oh, really?" asked Mr. Fitzroy sarcastically. "Perhaps you saw the miniseries?"

"Of course I haven't watched the miniseries! I have about a hundred pages to go."

"I doubt that," Mr. Fitzroy said. "*Pride and Prejudice* is far too sophisticated—"

"But I *am* reading it!" June said. "I've been homeschooled, and—"

"Aha!" Mr. Fitzroy said triumphantly. "A homeschooler!"

"A homeschooler and a reader," June insisted.

"You'll have plenty of time to read in detention." Mr. Fitzroy waved his hand as if he was brushing her away. "Please take your seat."

"Detention!" June stared at him. She had just gotten here! The class had gone very quiet; most of the kids were looking down, suddenly absorbed in their notebooks. The back row lifted their heads for the first time, and from his desk in the middle row, the boy named Joe looked straight at her. They locked eyes for a moment.

"Detention," Mr. Fitzroy said, returning to his desk as June got back into her seat in the front row. "Starting this afternoon through the end of the week."

"But—" June began, but Mr. Fitzroy talked right over her. "For tardiness, lack of preparation, and"—he looked at her significantly—"unruly behavior in the classroom."

June pressed her lips together. She realized she had been clutching her notebook so hard that the cover was bent over like a bow. She looked back at Mr. Fitzroy without saying a word. First class, first enemy. This was English, which she'd hoped would have some of the things she liked the most.

She loved to read; why couldn't he see that? A lump started in her throat. The truth was she had wanted to be wrong about school, and as a former stationery heiress, she admired the matching pencils and binders the girls had in the front row. It was so unfair. She felt like kicking over her stupid little desk and walking out of this place in a blaze of glory. Then she remembered that Indigo was waiting for her at home. Who knew what Aunt Bridget might do to him if she got thrown out of school? And if she was kept late and missed the bus, how would she ever get back to the farm? She didn't even know her own address.

"Everyone please get out your notebooks," said Mr. Fitzroy, and June picked up her pencil. She spent the rest of class drawing a long skyline sideways along the left margin: the Chrysler Building, the Empire State Building, and the Dakota. Just before the bell rang, she added clouds floating above the buildings in the shape of pigs and girls in pink tulle dresses.

8
Detention

Even though she had never been to school before, June knew what detention was, but in her mind the word transformed into "dungeon." She walked into the classroom fully expecting to see bars on the windows and instruments of torture hanging from the walls, but it was a whole lot less interesting than that. There were desks and fluorescent lights, a few other kids, and Mr. Fitzroy sitting at the front of the room. He didn't say anything when June came in, just checked off her name in a book on his desk and went back to his laptop, which was open to Facebook. Most of the other kids were either on laptops or phones, and nobody gave her a second glance, or even a first one.

June found a desk at the back of the room and did her homework quickly. She liked math but wasn't familiar with this workbook and wished she could ask someone in the room if she was on the right track, but everyone was so absorbed in their devices that Mr. Fitzroy didn't even have to ask them to be quiet. June looked at the clock: forty-five minutes to go. There were no windows in this classroom, but June figured that it must be getting dark out. What must Indigo be thinking? How would Aunt Bridget find out? She'd probably be forced to sleep in the barn tonight, June thought, and shuddered as she remembered the chopping block.

Just thinking about it made June want to bolt, but worrying about Indigo wouldn't get her home any faster, and getting into more trouble could only make things worse. She scanned the room again, looking for anything to distract her. There was a bookshelf with a lot of empty space. June went over to look at the books, wondering if people were allowed to get up from their desks during detention, but Mr. Fitzroy didn't seem to notice. There were two copies of *Consumer Reports* and four copies of *Chicken Soup for the Soul: Teens Talk Middle School.* She grabbed one of those and settled down to read. Maybe there was a chapter on how to survive a mean teacher.

A ball of paper landed on her desk. June looked up. It was Joe. Why hadn't she noticed him at the beginning? She opened the note: *I like those books.*

She looked up, wondering if he was being snarky, but he gave her a tentative smile. She wrote, *I can't decide if I love it or hate it*, balled up the paper, glanced at Mr. Fitzroy, then tossed it back. It landed on the floor near Joe, who quickly scooped it up and read it. This time he grinned and nodded. June smiled back, her first real smile of the whole day. Passing notes in school was the best part so far. Maybe she would end up sitting in the back row with the bad kids despite her good intentions.

A girl with brown hair braided intricately along both sides of her head looked over at them curiously.

Who are you? she mouthed.

June Sparrow, June mouthed back, too afraid to whisper aloud. *I like your braids,* June mouthed again, patting the side of her head. Maybe this girl could teach June to do her own hair like that.

Just then the door burst open and Aunt Bridget strode in. She was wearing mud-caked rubber boots, and her hair was sticking up all over her head. Everyone stared. June cringed.

Mr. Fitzroy got up from his desk. "Excuse me?"

"Don't you start with me, Henry," Aunt Bridget said. "I'm here to pick up my niece. June, come along."

"Your—" Mr. Fitzroy started, but Aunt Bridget cut him off.

"Yes, my niece." She nodded at June. "Gather your things."

June started cramming books into her bag.

"My niece, June Sparrow," Aunt Bridget continued. "Whom you saw fit to put into detention on her very first day at this school."

"Now, Bridget——" Mr. Fitzroy began.

Bridget? Henry? What was going on here?

"I don't care what she was doing, or what she may have said to you," Aunt Bridget declared, hands on hips. "It's her first day, and she doesn't need to be greeted with a punishment." She turned to June.

"Did you cut class?" she asked. June shook her head.

"Did you write bad words on a bathroom stall?" June shook her head.

"Did you set fire to a wastebasket?" June shook her head.

"Well, then." Aunt Bridget turned back to Mr. Fitzroy with a triumphant look. "You have already behaved far better than your teacher did when *he* was in middle school!"

Mr. Fitzroy's mouth was literally open in shock. June had an irresistible impulse to laugh—*almost* irresistible. She didn't dare look at any of the other kids or she would lose it.

"Come along, June," Aunt Bridget said. June ducked her head so Mr. Fitzroy wouldn't see her smile and followed her aunt out the door.

The Cadillac was still warm when June slipped into the passenger seat. Aunt Bridget turned the key and rolled down the window.

"Idiot!" she said as they pulled out of the school parking lot. "Henry Fitzroy was born an idiot and will die an idiot."

June giggled, and her aunt gave her a look. "And what do you have to laugh about, Missy? Ending up in detention your first day! Minnie told me about it when you didn't get off the bus."

"Who's Minnie?"

"Who's Minnie? Your bus driver, of course. Minnie Mileto—known her since grade school."

"You know everybody."

"Can't help that since I never went anywhere."

June wanted to ask why Aunt Bridget had never gone anywhere, but was scared she might get on her bad side again.

"I didn't do anything for detention," June said.

"I told Mr. Fitzroy that I had been reading *Pride and Prejudice* this summer, and he didn't believe me."

"I'm not surprised." Aunt Bridget stepped harder on the gas though the speedometer was already well over seventy-five miles per hour. "I doubt that Henry Fitzroy ever read anything past the South Dakota driver's manual. I was there the day he failed his driver's test—for the second time."

June laughed, and even though Aunt Bridget didn't take her eyes off the road, June was pretty sure she saw the hint of a smile.

As soon as they got home, June ran to find Indigo. It was dark inside the barn, and the bare lightbulbs threw thick, barred shadows of the rafters onto the dirt floor.

"Indigo? Indigo?" She waited to hear his scampering feet. Nothing.

She peered over the door of the stall where they had slept the night before. Then took a deep breath and turned to look at the chopping block.

Nothing.

June ran from stall to stall with her heart in her

throat, not caring if she frightened the horse and the cow, who rolled their eyes and stamped their hooves. The goat shook his little horns as if he wanted to pin her against the wall.

"Indigo!" she wailed. They had never been apart before; maybe Aunt Bridget had done something terrible to him! Or he had gone off to try to find June! But school was miles away, and if Indigo stayed out all night, he could freeze to death—or get run over by a car . . . or worse.

June ran back to the house. She would make Aunt Bridget go looking for Indigo; she would call the police; she would walk the fields all night with a flashlight if she had to! She slammed through the back door, not bothering to kick off her mud-caked ballet flats. "Aunt Bridget!" she yelled. "Indigo's gone! I can't find him out there! We have to—" She stopped dead. Right in front of the big metal gas heater was Indigo Bunting, sprawled out on a pink towel. He opened his eyes as June entered the room, but didn't move. Hot air ruffled the soft white down on his exposed belly.

June took him in her arms, her eyes filled with tears. She didn't know what was going on, but she had been so afraid that she couldn't speak a word. Indigo snuffled into her ear and began licking her face.

"Seemed like the critter was getting cold," Aunt Bridget said from the doorway into the kitchen. "Went out to muck the stalls this morning and he looked half froze. So I figured he could stay in here just for a little while."

"Thank you," June murmured into Indigo's soft pelt. "Thank you so much."

Aunt Bridget snorted and turned back to the kitchen. "Don't like house pets, you know. An animal's got to earn its keep on a farm."

"Oh, he will!" June said, kissing the pink-and-black spot right on the top of his head. "He'll work like crazy, you'll see! We both will!"

Indigo raised an eyebrow at this and Aunt Bridget said over her shoulder, "He may not be a messy eater, but what about when he needs to do his business? It's cold in the barn, but he's a pig, understand me? I don't want a mess in this house."

"In the apartment we used a litter box," June started, but Indigo squirmed out of her arms, marched right into the kitchen, and scratched purposefully at the back door, with a significant look at Aunt Bridget.

Aunt Bridget looked at him skeptically but opened the door, and Indigo trotted right outside with his curly tail in the air. "Well . . . ," Aunt Bridget said, turning to June, who had followed Indigo into the kitchen. "As long as he behaves like a gentleman."

"Oh, he will," said June. "Indigo Bunting is nothing if not a gentleman."

When June went up to bed that night, cradling Indigo in her arms, she was happy for the first time. "It's only our second night," she whispered to Indigo on the upstairs landing, "and you're already in the house with me!" Indigo licked her ear. "Okay, okay, you can act like you knew it all along, but really, Indigo, it's a miracle! You charmed Aunt Bridget!" She could swear that the quivering in his little body was from laughter. They went into her room and settled onto the bed. Indigo curled up in the crook of her arm like he always did, but June wasn't tired. It was the weekend, and she wouldn't have to face Mr. Fitzroy or the rest of them for two whole days. Two days had to be enough time to figure out how to get home to New York.

She turned on an old transistor radio that was next to the bed, and to her surprise it worked. She fiddled with the dials, and after spinning through some religious talk stations she found one that was playing country music. She didn't really like country music, but she liked the dramatic story lines: all lost loves and cheating hearts.

She settled back on her pillows and stared at the ceiling. There was a long crack that went just about the length of her bed. She looked more closely. This crack was outlined in pencil. It was faded, but she could see that someone had drawn all along the crack, outlining the break in the plaster. June stood up on the bed to get even closer to the ceiling. Now she could see that the crack had been turned into a mountain range, with other mountains drawn behind it, getting smaller in the distance. Tiny pine trees dotted the slopes, with a stream leading down through a valley and a crescent moon just coming up behind the peaks.

June touched the faded pencil marks. It was a funny feeling, knowing that this was where her mother had slept every night before June was born, before she met June's father, before anything had really happened. June plopped down on the bed again, waking Indigo, who had started snoring as soon as his head hit the pillow. He looked at her irritably.

"No, Indigo, this is important," June said. "Maybe things *had* happened already, even though she hadn't met Dad and started having this big glamorous life." Indigo looked quizzical. "I mean—what was it like? What was it really like to be her?"

June jumped off the bed and opened the closet door, pulling over the desk chair so that she could look at the top shelves, which were messy and crowded with an old Walkman CD player, headphones, and shoe boxes. A stack of CDs tumbled onto the floor as June tried to reach the first box.

"What's going on in there?" yelled Aunt Bridget, who was (of course) already in bed with the lights out.

"Nothing!" June called back. There was a beat, and Indigo glared at her. "I know, I know we're on probation," June whispered at him. He glared harder. "Okay, *you're* on probation." He snorted.

"Turn off that radio!" yelled Aunt Bridget.

"Yes, Aunt Bridget," June called. She climbed down to turn it off, and Indigo settled onto her pillow. After a few minutes June tiptoed over to the closet again. Indigo made an anxious whining noise down in his throat, but she didn't look back. She climbed on top of the chair and pulled down a shoe box that had the word PRIVATE written in black marker on the end of the box.

"Well, I guess we'll start here," she said, and brought it back to the bed. There was more writing on the top of the shoe box:

DO NOT OPEN ON PAIN OF LEGAL ACTION: THE KIND YOU DO NOT WANT

June smiled. Her mom was funny.

Indigo scooted up next to her and placed his trotters on the lid next to her hands. He looked at her questioningly.

"Of course we're going to open it," June said. "What does it matter now? This was all a really, really long time ago." Indigo shrugged and removed his trotters from the lid, waiting.

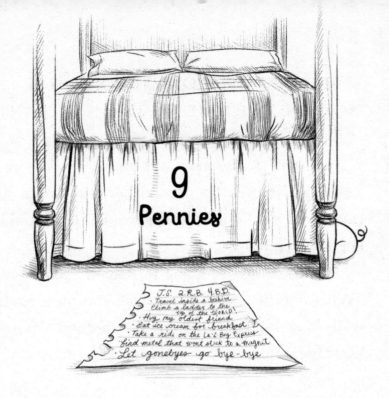

Inside the shoe box was a cream-colored spiral note-book, but when June pulled it out, it felt strangely heavy. June sat cross-legged on the bed, with Indigo resting his head on her leg, and opened the notebook. On the inside of the front cover she read:

I don't want anybody EVER EVER EVER to read this book! It is my own private Penny Book, and I will personally kill ANYBODY

who takes it away. SIGNED IN BLOOD!
(Well, not really.)

It wasn't filled with pictures of boys she had a crush on; it wasn't a scrapbook of a trip to the Grand Canyon: it was pennies. Page after page of pennies, and on the very first page were pennies glued to form letters spelling out MY PENNY BOOK. June looked up at the bedroom wall to the pennies glued there as well. So her mother was a coin collector from the beginning? A major teenage nerd. June would rather have seen pictures from her mother's prom night or even drooling baby pictures. She turned the page, there was some writing next to a penny taped in the upper right-hand corner:

November 17, 1999. Penny found on steps on the way into school. I had a math test today. I have a pimple the size of Mount Rushmore. I wish I lived in New York City.

New York City! Now, this was getting a little more interesting! The penny itself was circled in pencil with an arrow pointing at it, with another date scrawled next to it: 1972!

1972 Penny: In 1972 I wasn't even born. President Nixon was elected. Then he had to resign a couple years later because of Watergate. In 1972 there were demonstrations against the Vietnam War in places like San Francisco and NEW YORK CITY.

What was all this about New York? June wondered. Of course June wanted to go home, but her mom hadn't even moved there yet. Then she remembered the CDs that had fallen out of the closet and the rock-band poster on the back of the door. Maybe her mother had been a punk rocker! The punks all lived in the East Village in the eighties, so maybe that was it. But why had she hated her life in 1999?

June did the math: her mom was born in 1982, so she would have been seventeen years old. No wonder she hated her life: she was in high school in this same town, living in this same house and sleeping in this very same bedroom. June liked the bedroom, but she would have hated her life too. Luckily, this was not going to be June's life for too much longer. Somehow, some way, she and Indigo were going home.

June flipped more pages, and each one had the same thing: a penny taped to the upper right-hand corner and two entries. One was a short description of the day her mother had found the penny, and the other told some facts or memories about the year of the penny. Some of the pennies were really old, from before her mom was born, and sometimes she wrote what the old ones were worth next to the penny, though it was never very much, maybe one or two dollars. Of course, that was one or two hundred times more than a single penny was worth, but it still didn't seem worth getting too excited about.

November 25: It's Thanksgiving, so I don't have much time to write. Bob had to go to Sioux Falls to be with his aunt and uncle, so it's even more

boring here. But we're looking for the Big One!
Maybe he'll find it there. We now have $327.00,
and if I can only get Bob to say YES, we could
go to New York RIGHT NOW.
!!
!!!

The Big One! What was that? And who was
Bob? Her boyfriend? June reread the memory of the
day. It was pretty cool to know what her mom had
been thinking back when she was a teenager right
here in this very bedroom. It was even better than
a diary, because who really kept a diary for long?
June had started several diaries, but even though
she liked the kind that came with a little lock and
key, she could never stick with it. Her mom's Penny
Book seemed like a lot less work and a lot more fun.
The penny on this page was circled in red marker:

1960 Penny: Not the Big One, but this is special
because it's the year that President Kennedy was
elected. Back in the sixties Bob's family turned

their storm cellar into a bomb shelter with cans of
Spam and baked beans. It's still like that. Gross.

Okay, who was Bob? June's dad's name was
Jimmy. Jimmy and Roseanne Sparrow—June liked
the sound of that; names like that belonged in the
Country Music Hall of Fame. Bob and Roseanne
sounded awful. June herself would never date anyone named Bob. How utterly *boring*! But then again,
this was high school and maybe her mom had been
desperate. She was such a nerd.

December 25, 1999. Christmas Day
Bridget tried to make Dad's special waffles and
bacon as a treat this morning. Then she stole the
second piece of bacon off my plate. She is a senior
and pretty and popular. It's kind of hard not to
be jealous even on Christmas when she's trying to
make it nice for us. I miss Mom and Dad. I also
got two pennies to put into loafers. I am going to
tape them here instead, and I hope that counts even
though I didn't find them myself. Penny loafers

are cool and vintage I guess, but I don't have the loafers yet, just the pennies. Bridget ordered the loafers from a catalog. I already have my Converse high-tops and wear my cowboy boots most of the time. But it was really sweet of her. Problem is that it's extra sad to be sad on Christmas.

Aunt Bridget had been pretty and popular? Her mother had been jealous of her? Not June's glamorous mother, who flew around the world with her handsome husband, lived in New York, and went out every night of the week! Her mother was the one everyone was jealous of, not Aunt Bridget with her baggy old sweaters and rubber boots. June thought about the photograph in the hallway of the two of them. They had certainly both been pretty back then, and they looked happy. What happened? Was it because their parents died and Aunt Bridget was the oldest? But why hadn't she ever met Aunt Bridget before, and why didn't Aunt Bridget have her own family? Aunt Bridget had said that she never went anywhere, but did she really mean *anywhere*?

June read the entry again, looking for clues. She agreed with her mom: it *was* extra sad to be sad on Christmas. June often felt a little lonely on Christmas, though she went to *The Nutcracker* with Indigo Bunting and then home to watch *It's a Wonderful Life* and cry into her takeout Chinese food—which was an absolutely perfect Christmas as far as she was concerned. But the season could feel out of sync when you were surrounded by all these images of families that did not have the constellation of an orphan girl and a miniature pig. The good thing about New York was that you didn't have to be traditional about anything, so it felt less lonely when your family photos didn't match up.

June turned the next page and stared—it was torn in half! The part of the page where the penny had been taped was ripped right out of the book. There was nothing there to even tell the year of the penny. June quickly read the diary entry:

February 25, 2000: My 18th birthday! I found it! THE BIG ONE! I can't even write because I am supposed to go have cake and ice cream, but THIS IS IT! New York City, here we come! I am meeting Bob at the bank tomorrow and we are getting on the bus! In New York we'll go to the coin dealer first off. THE BIG ONE!!! I found it at the This 'n' That shop, right in the crack between the boards by the register. I only told Bob. THE BIG ONE!!!

The next page was blank. The page after it was ripped out. So were the next and the next! June flipped through the stubs of the missing pages. Nothing! The pages started up again close to the back of the album, but they were blank. Then she finally saw a penny taped in the corner:

I met a guy named Jimmy at the movie theater today. He gave me this penny. It's a new-minted 2000. Which is right now.

Jimmy! That had to be her dad! *2000 is right now.* . . . What about going to New York with Bob and cashing in the Big One? Where *was* the Big One, and why hadn't her mother written anything else? Some more pages were ripped out after the one about meeting Jimmy, and there was a big gap in the Penny Book. What happened to the Big One? What had happened to make her mom stop writing? Or maybe she hadn't stopped writing at all, but for some reason she decided to rip out the pages.

June ran her finger along the ripped edge at the binding of the book, and suddenly she remembered something. She reached for her purse, which she had shoved under the bed when she'd first arrived. There was her birthday penny, and inside the ziplock bag from Mr. Mendax was the piece of paper she was looking for: her mother's list. She spread the piece of paper out inside the notebook on her lap. Then June stopped breathing.

It matched. The ragged edge on the left side of the paper was exactly the same color and height as this notebook. This page had definitely been ripped out of the Penny Book!

"Look, Indigo," she whispered. "This means . . .
it means . . ."

Indigo looked confused.

"You're right. I don't know what it means." June
studied the list.

"If we're right about J.S. standing for June
Sparrow," June said quietly, "then Mom must have
written this list after I was born. But the paper
matches, so that means she took at least one of the
ripped-out pages from the Penny Book with her.
And if she wrote this crazy list on one of the missing pages, maybe she did something special with the
other ones. Maybe—maybe one of the other missing
pages has the Big One still taped on it!" She grabbed
Indigo and hugged him so hard, he squeaked. "Oh,
Indigo! That penny could be our ticket home!"

Indigo perched on the pillow next to her as June
read the whole list over again:

J.S. 2 R.B. 4 B.D.
Travel inside a beehive
Climb a ladder to the top of the world

Hug my oldest friend
Eat ice cream for breakfast
Take a ride on the La-Z-Boy express
Find metal that won't stick to a magnet
Let gonebyes go bye-bye

June sighed. Indigo sighed. None of it really made sense except for "J.S." Then June turned over the paper and saw something that made her literally gasp out loud. There was a hand-drawn red circle the exact size of penny. She could still see the remains of Scotch tape stuck around it. She hadn't even known what that meant before!

But there was no penny. No diary entry. No Big One.

June quickly flipped back to the beginning of the Penny Book.

"Come on, Indigo," she said. "We'll read the whole thing over again from the beginning. There has to be a clue in here somewhere."

The door slammed open and June jumped off the bed. The Penny Book and Indigo Bunting both tumbled to the floor. Indigo disappeared under the bed so fast there was only a blur of curly tail. Aunt Bridget towered in the doorway. She had on a long, flowery nightgown that seemed like the last thing Aunt Bridget would wear. June wouldn't have been surprised if she went to sleep with her rubber boots sticking out the end.

"What are you doing!"Aunt Bridget swooped in and grabbed the Penny Book before June could make a move. "Reading your mother's diary? Poking and prying into other people's business at one o'clock in the morning? Not in this house!"

Aunt Bridget slammed the closet door shut with a loud bang. She had been angry with Mr. Fitzroy in detention, but this was a new level of outrage. Maybe Aunt Bridget was a Jekyll and Hyde; maybe if she got woken up in the middle of the night; maybe when the moon was full—

Aunt Bridget whirled back to face June, the Penny Book clutched tightly to her chest. "Do you hear me, young lady?"

"Pretty hard not to!" June snapped back.

"How dare you start sneaking around, staying up all night—"

"I wasn't sneaking! She's my mother, and everything of hers belongs to me!"

"Not everything!" Aunt Bridget said. "Not everything belongs to *you*, I'll have you know. While you're in my house you'll follow my rules, understood?"

June bit her lip. She was a prisoner here, at least for now.

"I can read her diary if I want to," June said more evenly.

"No." Aunt Bridget stepped toward the bedroom door. "It's not her diary; it's her Penny Book. And no, you can't." June jumped off the bed and followed her aunt down the hallway onto the second-floor landing with its worn blue carpeting.

"It's not fair!" June yelled. Aunt Bridget kept walking into her bedroom and closed the door without bothering to turn around. June ran after her and tugged at the door, but Aunt Bridget had locked it from the inside. Something cracked inside her, and June pounded on the door, screaming at the top of her lungs, "It's mine! Give it back! That book belongs to me! She's my mother! Give it back!" And finally, "I hate you!"

She yelled and kicked at the door, the sound echoing inside the silence of that wooden house, which creaked every time anyone took a step. But you can only yell insults for so long when nobody yells back. You can only pound on a door for so long when nobody opens it. Eventually June slumped to the floor, and looking past the hallway night-light, she saw Indigo poking his head out of her bedroom, worried. June felt dizzy, and her throat was raw with yelling. She held out her arms, and Indigo scampered down the hall and squirmed onto her lap. She hugged him as he burrowed his head into her shoulder, but this was the kind of sadness that even Indigo couldn't help her with. This time she felt too sad to cry. June pushed herself slowly to her feet, carried Indigo into bed with her, and tucked them both under the covers. She looked out the window at the tree branches moving back and forth against this strange midwestern night until the light began to come up and the landscape turned back into something recognizable. Indigo snored next to her inside her mother's pink room, and she watched the horizon turn an even brighter pink.

When June was home in New York, it seemed like things flowed along just like they were supposed to. Now that she was stuck in South Dakota, it was so much harder not to be able to ask her mom any questions. June felt for the list still safely in her pocket. At least Aunt Bridget hadn't seen that. Was it a birthday list? A bucket list? Why had her mother kept it in her wallet, and why was it written on a torn-out page from the Penny Book?

She reached for her purse, which had fallen behind the bed when Aunt Bridget came bursting in, and pulled out the plastic case with her birthday penny inside. Then she fished around for the small photo of her mother holding her as a baby. June took the photo and leaned it against the bedside lamp. She held her birthday penny tightly in her fist, looked at the picture of her mom, and whispered, "Why? Why? Why?"

10
This 'n' That

When Aunt Bridget called June down for breakfast, June realized that she had better apologize. June had done a lot of thinking and only a tiny bit of sleeping the night before. She had to make life bearable for as long as she and Indigo were trapped there, which looked like it might be longer than she thought. June was still angry—in fact, she was more than angry—she was outraged that Aunt Bridget had taken something of her mother's away from her. But she had to play her cards right so that

it the night before, even though she knew she was in the right. She would have to sneak into Aunt Bridget's room to look for the Penny Book, but couldn't risk that this morning—better to wait until Aunt Bridget wasn't home. June took her time washing the dishes and the oatmeal pot, then pulled on her mother's hat and scarf and stepped into the muddy boots she had left on the front porch, which were dry but felt wet because the rubber was so cold.

Aunt Bridget was milking the goat (who knew that girl goats also had horns and goatees?). She had left all the feeding and cleaning out of stalls for June. There were coffee cans in bins of grain and piles of loose hay that had to be pitched into the feeding racks for the horse and the cow. The manure had to be raked up and wheelbarrowed out to a large pile outside the barn door that was half covered by a big blue tarp. Aunt Bridget supervised her but didn't actually lend a hand with anything, and June got the distinct feeling that this was the only time she was going to be shown how to do this—the next time she would be on her own.

"You're not ready for milking yet," Aunt Bridget said, watching June maneuver nervously around the horse so she could clean his stall. The goat was tethered in the center of the barn and narrowed her yellow eyes as June tugged on the halter of Mr. Chips, who seemed determined not to leave the barn without his goat friend. I'll never be ready for milking, June thought as Mr. Chips leaned his formidable weight in the opposite direction.

Aunt Bridget reached over without even looking and slapped Mr. Chips's backside with the flat of her hand. He took off out the door so fast that June lost her footing, let go of the halter, and ended up with a mixture of dirt and hay down the back of her pants and inside her boots. She thought she saw Aunt Bridget grin as June pulled hay out of the top of her pants, but she couldn't be absolutely certain. June wasn't speaking to her aunt—but unfortunately, it didn't seem like Aunt Bridget even noticed.

Indigo Bunting, on the other hand, was having the time of his life. He trotted from stall to stall as if he was the mayor, sniffing and wagging his curly little tail. Traitor, thought June, as she carried a shovelful of manure past where he had perched himself on a nice dry nest of hay. One day here and he knows everybody. She glared at him and he gave her a sweet smile. She threw the manure with such force that it went flying off the shovel and landed with a loud splat on the side of the barn.

Someone started laughing in a deep voice, and June spun around to see a farmer dressed exactly like Aunt Bridget, plus red suspenders. He had come around the side of the barn just in time to get some of the manure onto his wide, flannel-shirted front. He pulled a bandanna from his back pocket and wiped his shirt clean, still laughing. June wondered if everyone in South Dakota found it amusing to get splattered with horse poop.

"I'm sorry," she said quickly. "Really, really sorry."

He raised his eyebrows at her but didn't look angry at all. "And you are?"

"June." She felt horribly embarrassed. What a way to meet someone! "Really, I am so sorry, sir—"

"No, no, it's fine." He shook his head, smiling. "These are my farm clothes. Actually, they're my only clothes except for my funeral clothes." He laughed again and held out his hand. "Bob Burgess."

"June Sparrow." She gave him a good firm handshake, hoping this might make a better impression. But as soon as she said her full name, his smile faded and he stepped back.

"Sparrow?"

"I see you've met my niece." Aunt Bridget stepped out of the shadow of the barn door.

"Niece?" If all he can do is repeat what people say to him, June thought, maybe he's a little slow on the uptake.

"Roseanne's daughter," Aunt Bridget said carefully, without expression. She turned to June. "Bob is our nearest neighbor, next farm over."

Bob . . . *Bob!* June froze. *She* was the slow one! This was the same Bob from her mom's Penny Book—it had to be! Her first boyfriend, the one she collected pennies with, and he still lived next door!

(Didn't anybody ever leave home around here?)

"You collected pennies with my mom!" she said. Bob took another step back and stared at her.

"How did you know that?" he asked.

"I found her Penny Book! It talked all about you, and going to New York and—"

"That's enough," Aunt Bridget broke in. "That was all a long time ago. Don't pay her any mind, Bob."

"You have Roseanne's Penny Book?" he asked quietly, staring harder than ever at June.

"I found it last night." June looked at Aunt Bridget, waiting for her to explain. But Aunt Bridget said nothing, and June looked back at Bob. He was blushing so hard that his ears turned red. "May I please show it to him, Aunt Bridget?" June asked as politely as she could. Maybe she could trap Aunt Bridget into bringing it out; then she could just grab it and run.

"It's not here," Aunt Bridget said abruptly.

"What do you mean? You took it last night. It's in your room."

"No, it's not," Aunt Bridget said in a strained voice. "I dropped it off at the This 'n' That shop's collection box early this morning, along with a bunch of other junk we don't need around here anymore."

"No!" June exploded. "How dare you? What collection box? That belonged to my mom, not you! Get it back!"

"I can't," Aunt Bridget said. "That box stays locked up to the public. You can put things in but you don't take things out. It's gone, girl. Forget it."

June stared at Aunt Bridget, too angry to speak. Then she turned to Bob. "Where's the This 'n' That shop?"

"It's downtown," he stammered. "But your aunt is right—"

"It's *my* Penny Book! Everything of my mother's belongs to me!" June said, looking from one to the other. Indigo had trotted out when he heard raised voices, and now he shoved his nose against her shin. June leaned down and grabbed him. "Come on, Indigo. We're going downtown."

"And exactly how are you going to get there?" Aunt Bridget asked. "You think you can just hail a cab at the end of the driveway? This is not Fifth Avenue, Missy."

June narrowed her eyes. She had never, *ever* hated anyone as much as she hated Aunt Bridget.

"I'll walk," she said coldly. "We walk a lot in New York City. I'm used to it."

She turned on her crusted boot heels and headed for the driveway.

It was a good exit, but just before she reached the corner of the barn, she thought of something and turned back.

"What happened to the Big One?" she asked Bob. He looked at her, then at Aunt Bridget. June didn't think his face could get any more pink, but it did. A pinkish purple all the way from his forehead to where his chest disappeared under his blue plaid shirt.

"It was a long time ago," he said, looking back at Aunt Bridget and then down at his boots.

"Hmmph!" snorted June.

"Hmmph!" snorted Indigo Bunting from her arms, and they headed down the driveway to start the long trek into town.

11

Moses

For a while rage fueled her march down the high-way, but when that ran out, June hit a wall of pure exhaustion. To be honest, she wasn't one hundred percent sure that she was walking in the right direc-tion. In Manhattan it was easy: the numbers went down when you went downtown and up when you went uptown. South Dakota looked all the same to her, the road a straight line through high fields of cornstalks and fewer trees than she used to see out her window overlooking Central Park. What did this place have to do with June Sparrow?

Then she remembered her mother's mysterious list in her pocket and the Penny Book tossed into a drop box, and kept walking. There was something Aunt Bridget didn't want her to find out about the Penny Book, and Bob had something to do with it; that much was obvious. No matter what they were trying to hide—the Big One?—June wasn't about to let Aunt Bridget decide which of her mother's things she was allowed to keep. June snorted indignantly, her breath clouding white in the cold air. Someone had once told her that twenty New York City blocks equals one mile. She used to walk forty or fifty blocks when the weather was fine, strolling along the Hudson River just for the fun of it. She could surely walk a couple of miles into town. Indigo Bunting was tucked against her waist inside her jacket, which made a little carrying pouch for him when she zipped it up. She could go faster this way, but not for the first time she wished that he could walk beside her.

She had almost never felt lonely in New York;

being surrounded by so many different lives had made her feel part of a big extended family. Someone was always cooking, playing music, arguing, making up, watching a movie . . . All these parallel lives were comforting. Plus, it was so quiet in South Dakota; no wonder she couldn't sleep at night. No sirens, no late-night talking or laughter drifting up from the street to influence her dreams. Here there was only wind and more wind.

As if to prove her wrong, the rattling cough of an engine sounded behind her. She had been walking for about half an hour without seeing any cars. A gray pickup truck with a camper on the back was coming toward her. At least she thought it was gray, but when it got closer she saw that the front grille was silver and the fenders were red. Not a shiny red—nothing on this truck was shiny. Then she realized that the truck was slowing down; in fact, it was stopping right in front of her. The truck came to a shuddering halt, and now she could see a little wooden cabin built onto the back of the pickup with a door facing the rear. It had a curved roof and a window on the side complete with a window box filled with flowers. There was even a black stovepipe coming out of the roof. June took a big step away from the truck.

Maybe this was one of those people Shirley Rosenbloom was always warning her about: Stranger Danger Alert! June quickly unzipped her jacket and held Indigo straight out in front of her— she hoped that he could bite if he had to, though he had been snoozing away in the warmth of her jacket, and now he looked utterly confused at being thrust out into the cold, eyes heavy with sleep.

"Act like a guard dog," June whispered fiercely as the driver leaned across and popped open the passenger door. Indigo yawned widely and June gave him a shake. This was life or death!

The man inside the truck leaned over so that he could see her clearly. "Want a ride?" he asked. He was not a very young man and he was not a very large man. In fact, he was a little old man. His face was very wrinkled, but there was something about him that made him look younger. Maybe it was the way his whole face seemed to smile. He was wearing a quilted farm jacket and a green baseball cap.

"No, thank you," June said. "We're fine."

The old man waited a moment. "I'm heading into town, and you look like you might need a ride."

"Nope," June said firmly. "No, thank you."

"Okay, then," he said, but the door remained open. His eyes were bright as he gazed at them and June realized she might look a little silly with Indigo Bunting held out in front of her like a dangling shield.

"That's a fine miniature pig you have there," the man said. "Excellent specimen of the breed."

June stared. She had never met anyone who knew what a miniature pig was before she told them. Usually they just assumed that Indigo was a new breed of dog, or a baby full-size pig. "Thank you," she said slowly.

"What's his name?"

"Indigo Bunting."

"Indigo Bunting! One of my favorite birds," he said, looking more closely at June.

"Are you a bird-watcher?" June asked before she could remember not to talk with strangers. Nobody knew that Indigo Bunting was a bird name.

"I do my best," he said. "I keep a notebook. What made you decide to name him after a bird?"

"I just liked the sound of it." June hoped that he wasn't going to laugh or think she was cute.

He didn't laugh. "My name is Moses," he said. "My parents weren't more religious than most, so maybe they just liked the sound of it too. Moses in the bullrushes, that's me, but I don't know a bullrush from a buffalo."

June smiled, though she hadn't meant to. The old man smiled back. "Sure you don't want a ride? I'm headed to the This 'n' That shop, but I can drop you pretty much anywhere."

"The This 'n' That shop? You know where the drop box is?" June's voice cracked, and Indigo squeaked as she tucked him back under her arm a little too hard.

"I ought to," Moses said. "I work there four days a week."

"Really? Thank you! I mean—yes, we would like a ride to town, to the drop box, that is. Thank you, sir." She and Indigo could certainly handle a little old man, June thought as she walked toward the pickup and clambered onto the high seat. This was meant to be! Who knew how long it would take for her to walk there, and he actually worked at the shop. . . . This was kismet (one of her favorite words), and she would be a fool to ignore it.

The first thing she noticed when she got into the truck was that it smelled sweet, but she couldn't place it. The second thing she noticed was a large bee buzzing against the windshield. June made a sound that was not exactly a shriek, but not exactly something else, and rolled down her window so that it would fly out.

"Wait a minute!" Moses said quickly. "We don't want to lose him."

"Lose him?" June started to brush the bee toward the window with a piece of newspaper.

"Now, cut that out." Moses held up a hand to

stop her. "You don't want to hurt him!"

"What are you talking about?" June put the newspaper back down on the seat but shrank back. The bee was banging against the ceiling and the windshield right in front of her face. "I hate bees!"

"Can't hate bees," Moses said very seriously as he reached across and rolled up the window. "They're too important to hate. Just settle down, and he'll settle down too."

So he *was* crazy. Well, at least she was getting a ride to the right place. June stopped moving, and it was true: the bee settled onto the big gray sun visor that served as a clipboard for a pile of papers stuck between the visor and the ceiling.

"The bees mostly stay in the back." Moses gestured with his thumb behind their seat. "They like to stay in the hive when we're moving."

June turned around to look, and Indigo stood on his hind legs to look over her shoulder. She couldn't see anything but the roof of the cabin and the window box.

"You have a beehive in the back?"

"Yep. Built it custom."

"I don't see any bees."

"They like to stay inside on the road. Very smart creatures, bees."

"Inside?"

"Inside the hive, not the truck." Moses laughed. Indigo and June looked at each other.

Travel inside a beehive.

It was the first thing on her mother's list!

"So, it's sort of like traveling inside a beehive, isn't it?" June tried to sound as casual as possible, but she knew that Indigo could feel her heart pounding through her jacket.

"Never thought of that!" Moses shook his head as if it was the most extraordinary thing he'd ever heard. "Traveling inside a beehive. I guess you're right. I just figured it was the easiest way to keep track of the bees."

June touched the front pocket of her jeans, where she had put the list this morning when she got dressed, but she didn't want to pull it out in front of Moses. What if the list was all about Red Bank? But if things in Red Bank were so important, why didn't her mother come back after she got married? Something big must have happened to make her stay away.

There was a loud buzz as the bee left its perch and careened past Indigo's nose. June pulled him back, terrified, but Moses chuckled. "I know you miss your buddies," he said to the bee. "You'll be reunited soon enough."

June checked behind her, a little worried that there might be a connecting vent between the cabin and the back of the truck. Indigo had never been stung by a bee, and June couldn't remember if she actually had or only felt like she had. This buzzing bumble had gotten into the front somehow . . . but she didn't see a beehive.

"What does a beehive look like?" she asked Moses. She wasn't about to tell him about the list or the Penny Book.

The old man laughed, and though June usually hated it when grown-ups laughed at her questions, this time it didn't make her feel like a little kid. Moses had a comfortable laugh that rolled along without rushing to get to the punch line. "How could you possibly know? I meant to sort of hide it in plain sight, if you know what I mean. People can get a little nervous around bees."

June and Indigo gave each other a look.

"It's right there under the window box," Moses said. "See how it's kind of built out in a square under there? That's the beehive."

June looked into the side mirror but she couldn't see a thing. The flowers in the window box fluttered in the wind, but there was no sign of a bee, a honeycomb, or even some stray beeswax dripping down the side of the truck. "Are those flowers real?" she asked.

"You know, that is the question I get asked the most," said Moses. "Not 'Did you build this yourself?' Not 'Do you live in this truck?' But 'Are the flowers real?'"

"Did you build it yourself? Do you live in this truck?" June asked.

Moses turned and looked at her, his hands holding steady on the big gray steering wheel. "The flowers are real."

12
The Drop Box

June wouldn't have known that she had entered the town of Red Bank except for the fact that the houses were built closer together and they didn't look much like farmhouses anymore. There were no traffic lights, and June figured she must be on Main Street when she saw a coffee shop and a hardware store. There was a woman in a brightly colored apron sweeping the sidewalk in front of a hardware store. She stopped sweeping to wave at Moses when he drove by.

"Agata is very particular about her sidewalk," said Moses. "That's Kazik's Hardware, more like a general store. They've got everything from baling wire to sewing needles."

A rack of clothes fluttered in the wind in front of the coffee shop, and two girls who looked about June's age were sitting in lawn chairs.

"There's my competition," he said. "Keisha and her twin sister set up their own 'vintage' clothes sale every Saturday." He smiled. "I don't really mind, of course; perks things up a bit on Main Street." Moses waved at them too, and the girls waved back.

"Does everybody wave here?" June asked.

Moses paused a moment. "Now, that's another thing I never thought about," he said. "I guess we do. Where are you from?"

"New York City." June felt that familiar tightness in her throat just from saying it out loud.

"People not so friendly there?"

"No, it's not that. . . ." How could she explain that despite their bad reputation, New Yorkers were very friendly? Sometimes *too* friendly! She was always getting stopped on the street by people who wanted to pat Indigo and ask all about him. "We're not big wavers," she said finally. "But New Yorkers love to talk!"

A boarded-up old movie house had the most impressive facade in town, and Moses began to whistle when they got close to it. June and Indigo exchanged looks, she could have sworn that he was whistling an aria from *La Bohème*.

"Do you like opera?" June asked a little shyly.

"I love opera!" Moses yanked his thumb toward the movie house. "That used to be the Vaudeville Palace before it turned into a movie theater. Opera companies still came to Red Bank when I was little, and I went to every single show. I did go to the opera once in Sioux Falls, and that was pretty good too."

June craned around in her seat to look. The Vaudeville Palace had cornices like curlicues and a tragedy/comedy mask sculpted over the entrance. June thought that the building looked like a grand old duchess all dressed up for a ball, somehow frozen in time.

"It's beautiful," June said, but she also thought it was a little sad.

"You should see the inside." Moses pulled the truck over in front of the boarded-up box office. "The ceiling is painted blue, with gilt cherubs and constellations that used to really light up in the old days."

"Do they show movies there now?"

"They shut down a couple of years ago," Moses said. "Guess it's hard to get people to leave their living rooms. Though honestly, I'm not sure why that is. What's so special about the living room?"

"I love going to the movies," said June. "And I *love* the opera."

Moses nodded in agreement as he drove the truck away from the movie house and whistled even louder.

They continued along Main Street toward a low metal building at the end of town with a silo towering over it. The silos dotting the landscape in South Dakota reminded June of the water towers that topped lots of buildings in New York City.

"That silo got shut down after there was a bad accident," Moses said as they passed.

"What happened?"

"A man was killed," Moses said quietly. "You've always got to be careful when you're working in a silo. Now, over there is the grain elevator." Moses pointed out a two-story extension to the building with "Coca-Cola" painted on the side. The lettering was so old, it looked like a movie set. "That's where they weighed it up and loaded it out. Those train tracks run directly into the building, and they could just fill up the freight cars with grain and haul them away. That was modern times."

"Do they still do that?"

"Not so much—not in this building, anyway." Moses drove past the back of the grain elevator, and June could see that the parking lot had grass sprouting through cracks in the asphalt.

"But there's plenty of farms, still," June said. "Nothing but farms."

"Nothing but," Moses repeated.

June realized that the houses were getting farther

apart now that they were past the silo and the grain elevator. They hadn't seen one other person after they passed the coffee shop and hardware store. The whole town seemed dusty and deserted, which made it look even more like an old movie or TV show, maybe a gunslinging Western.

"When are we getting downtown?" June asked.

"Oh, sweetheart." Moses grinned. "That *was* downtown. Now we're headed out again."

June turned around in her seat. "But there wasn't even a gas station."

"Nope." Moses swung the truck around to the left. "Gotta go to Masonville for gas. People used to have their own gas pumps on the farm, you know, for the machinery."

"Cool." June loved the idea of pumping her own private gas, not that she'd ever pumped gas in her life. "How come they don't anymore?"

"It's against the law." Moses parked the truck at the back of a one-story building with white siding. "Those gas tanks crack when they get old and make underground oil spills. Bad for the crops and bad for the bees. What's bad for them is bad for people too. The canary in the mine, that's what you are, my friend."

June realized that Moses was speaking to the bee on the visor, though she had no idea what he was talking about. The bee started buzzing around the cab again and June pulled Indigo close.

"It's all right." Moses pushed open his door with a loud squeak. "You can come out now, Floyd."

"Floyd? You name them? How can you tell them apart?" asked June as Floyd buzzed out the door.

"I can't," Moses whispered, as if he didn't want Floyd to hear him. "I call all of them Floyd, except for Her Majesty, of course."

"Her Majesty?"

"Her Majesty, the Queen."

June laughed and reached for the passenger door. Now that Floyd had left the vehicle, things felt a lot less risky. She knew that she was never supposed to get in a car with a stranger, but it wasn't her fault that you couldn't get a taxi around here.

June walked to the side of the truck. Now that she was closer, she saw the beehive built into the side of the truck under the window box. It was a fairly large rectangular box with a narrow opening at the bottom for the the bees, who were beginning to fly out. June tried not to panic, but she soon realized that all the Floyds seemed quite intent on getting to work and paid no attention to June and Indigo.

"That's a good smell, isn't it?" Moses called out from the other side of the truck. "Can you smell the honey?"

June could smell something—she just hadn't known what she was smelling. It wasn't exactly the same as honey from a jar; it was sweet and some-how warming, even though the day was cool.

"Leaping Liberace," June said slowly. She took a step closer, and Indigo sniffed loudly and put his nose in the air the way he did when she scratched behind his ears.

"Good, huh?" Moses said. He came around to their side of the truck and when June saw him she couldn't help but stare—Moses was in a wheelchair!

"You— You—" Indigo nudged her in the stomach. She didn't mean to be rude!

"I'm in a wheelchair." Moses smiled. "Surely they have those in New York City?"

June flushed. "Of course, I'm sorry, it's just that . . ." Moses didn't look offended, so she took a deep breath and went on. "You were driving."

"I've driven since I got my license at fifteen and a half, and I've been in a chair since I was five years old and got polio." Moses turned his chair around and went back to the driver's side. "Come over here and I'll show you how this rig works."

Moses opened the door and pointed at the steering wheel. "Do you know how to drive yet?"

"No," June said. "I've never even tried."

"Well, this truck is made special order for folks like me. See that handle next to the steering wheel? I can do everything with my hands: gas, brakes, the works!"

"I don't even know how to drive with hands *and* feet," said June.

"I'll tell you what's even better than being able

to drive with my hands," Moses said. "This wheel-chair carrier!"

Moses pointed out some hardware mounted behind the driver's seat. "I strap my chair in behind the seat when I'm driving. Then I can just take it down when I arrive. Those hooks are operated by remote control, so I just hook up the chair and guide it out. The motor lowers it out of the truck, no problem."

"No problem?" June asked.

"It's actually kind of fun." Moses reached up for a remote control that she now saw was attached by Velcro to the side of his seat. He pressed a button, and one of the straps started to lower so that he could reach it easily. "It works the same way in reverse. I can run the whole operation from the driver's seat. The wheelchair folds up and fits back there. I'll show you later if you'd like." Moses pressed another button, and the strap whirred back into place. Then Moses shut the door and turned his chair to face June. "I'm kind of like a turtle," he said. "I live in the cabin on the back of the truck, and keep everything I need right inside the shell. Designed the whole thing myself."

June and Indigo looked at each other, impressed. Moses wheeled around to the beehive and sat directly in front of it, watching the bees go in and out.

"That hive needs to be emptied pretty soon," Moses said, as June and Indigo joined him (keeping a few feet back from the bees). "Too much honey and they'll leave the hive. Swarm. Once a bee colony fills a hive with honey, they figure that their work is done. But they seem to like it here pretty well. It's the only mobile beehive in the state, far as I know."

June and Indigo looked at each other. It was true—they had just traveled inside a beehive. All of a sudden June felt like she had no time to lose.

She turned to Moses. "Where's the drop box?"

"Right over there." Moses pointed at a large metal box near the back door that looked like a giant's mailbox painted yellow instead of blue. June ran over with Indigo skittering behind her. She pulled on the handle, which opened easily. She went up on her tiptoes, but just like a real mailbox, it was pitch-dark inside. Moses was watering his window box with a small tin can attached to the truck by a string.

"How do I get inside?" June yelled across the parking lot. "I can't see anything!"

Moses didn't answer. She ran over to him, "Please, Moses. I have to get in there. Something of mine got put in there this morning and I have to get it back."

"Happens all the time," Moses said. "People don't clean their rooms, and Mom threatens she's going to put it in the trash. But of course, she doesn't—not the first time, not the second time, but the *third* time—"

"My mom's dead," June said flatly. "She and my dad both died when I was three."

Moses looked at June, then up at the clouds stretching a thin layer of horsetails across the sky. "There I go again, Moses the Bigmouth, rattling on when I don't know what the heck I'm talking about." He gave a big sigh and tugged on his suspenders, which hung loose against his shirt front. Moses looked June right in the eye. "Will you forgive me for being so foolish?"

"Of course, of course I will," she said, wishing he wouldn't make such a big deal about it. "They died a long time ago. It's just—" June stopped talking and Moses waited. She wasn't sure how much she wanted to tell him. "It's just that my mom's Penny Book got put in there by my aunt, without my permission, and I have to get it back."

"Her Penny Book?" Moses raised an eyebrow. He stowed the watering can inside a metal storage box built into the side of the truck. "See you later, Floyd," he said to the bees, and wheeled toward the back door of the building, pulling a ring of keys from his pocket. "We can get into the drop box, don't worry, in fact we have to—that's one of my jobs. Before I leave for the day, always sort through the drop box."

Moses went up the ramp and opened the back door of the shop, and when the light flicked on overhead, June saw a jumble of garbage bags with clothes spilling out under a long table. Moses gave her an embarrassed smile. "I'm not quite as meticulous as the bees, I'm afraid."

"It's fine," June said impatiently. "Please, Mr. Moses—"

"Moses. Everyone calls me Moses."

"Do you have a key to the drop box, sir? Moses? Can we just look?"

"Sure we can. I'll just open up the front—" He looked at her face. "Well, maybe we'll open a little late today."

It seemed to take forever for Moses to go back across the parking lot and fit another key from his enormous key ring into the slot at the back of the drop box, which opened the back like a miniature door. The lock was a little sticky, and Moses reached down to push against the bottom of the door in a familiar way to open it. Loose clothes were crammed on top of one another, along with a pair of boots, the mud still damp. Moses started piling everything into a plastic bin he had brought back out with him.

"Muddy boots?" June asked, when Moses tossed them to the side so that they wouldn't get mud on the clothes donations.

Moses shrugged. "Some people feel pretty free to leave strange things in a box in a parking lot." He glanced over at the boots, lying on their sides on the asphalt. "Nothing wrong with 'em. One wipe with a damp rag and they're good to go."

June started pulling clothes out, a little afraid of what she might find, but she wasn't about to let Moses do all the work. More clothes, a torn paper bag filled with plastic toys, another grocery bag with paperback mysteries spilling out, and toward the bottom a layer of pamphlets from the Jehovah's Witnesses.

"Do you resell all this?"

"We sort it, try to put it to good use. What we can't sell goes one place or another." He gave a sigh. "Some has to go to the dump in the end. But there's people picking over the dump as well, and lots of great finds end up in the town dump." He brightened. "That's where me and the Floyds park the truck every night, up the hill off Dump Road. People like to tease me about living at the dump, but I get first dibs on everything, and unless the wind's blowing wrong, it doesn't smell a bit!"

June had never been to a town dump in her life. In New York, at least at the Dakota, the garbage just sort of disappeared. Maybe it went to New Jersey or out to sea. Either way was kind of awful to think about, and it made her feel funny that she had never really thought about it before. They had reached the end of the pile of clothes and the drop box was empty. She started clawing through the bin again. Maybe she had missed the Penny Book, maybe . . . no.

She looked at Moses. "Aunt Bridget said she put it in here this morning."

"I'm sorry." Moses looked down at the pile of donations. "If she said this morning, it should be in here, that's for sure."

June froze. "She's a liar," she said slowly. "She's a liar and she hates me."

Indigo and Moses both looked shocked.

"She has to be lying!" June insisted. "It would be here. She just doesn't want me to have it because she hated my mother and she hates me."

"That's three 'hate's in a short amount of time," said Moses.

"Then why isn't it here?"

"I don't know," he said. "But I do know that you usually have to know someone pretty well to hate them. How long have you been living with your aunt?"

"Three days," said June.

Moses looked surprised. "I never got around to asking your name."

"June Sparrow. My aunt is Bridget Andersen."

"Of course! She lives on the farm out by where I picked you and your little buddy up."

June nodded. "I just got here."

Moses looked surprised. "All the way from New York City on your own? That's a long trip."

"Not that long," June said, but something about the way Moses was looking at her made her have to glance away. She stared at the pile of clothes in the bin.

"How about if you help me sort through this stuff and I'll make a couple of cups of Postum," said Moses. "I've got a kettle in there, and there's nothing like Postum on a cold morning."

"What's Postum?" June managed. There was an undeniable lump in her throat, and her voice didn't sound quite right.

"It's a brown liquid some of us drink around here instead of coffee," Moses said a little ruefully. "Not bad, though, when you add Carnation."

June looked at the empty drop box and then at Indigo, who was shivering. What did she have to lose when she'd already lost everything but him?

She wrapped her jacket around Indigo and followed Moses into the back of the store.

13
Joe Pye

The front of the store had racks of clothes and shelves with glassware and kitchenware. Along the side wall was a series of shoe racks where hard-worn cowboy boots tilted over onto almost new strappy sandals; children's sneakers and flip-flops were shoved in everywhere. Moses unlocked the front door and turned the "Closed" sign around on its string to "Open." He flipped on the lights and turned the thermostat up, but it was still cold inside the store.

"Grab a sweater," he said cheerfully, pointing at the clothes racks, and when June hesitated, he added, "Don't worry, you can work off the price." June felt a lot less cheerful than Moses when she looked through the clothes. Everything here looked huge, and she felt a little funny about looking through other people's used clothing.

Logically, it was exactly the same thing as shopping at a vintage store, but right now she was freezing and tired. Indigo hadn't stopped shivering since they got out of the truck. She stopped flipping hangers at a chunky black sweater with a big-eyed Dalmatian puppy appliquéd on the front. June held the sweater up against herself and looked in one of the mirrors that were nailed to the wall at random locations. The sweater hung almost to her knees and looked a little bit like a craft project that had gone on vacation to Disneyland. Maybe if she belted it . . . She had to smile just a little. Who was she trying to impress, anyway?

"Postum's ready!" called Moses from the back of the store.

June looked at Indigo for his opinion on the Dalmatian sweater, but he seemed oblivious to fashion for once, so she pulled it over her head. She had to admit it was cozy.

She wanted to sneak a look at the rest of her mother's list, which was still tucked safely in her pocket, but she didn't want Moses to wonder what she was doing. Besides, poor Indigo was so chilled that his snout was starting to drip, so she tucked him underneath the sweater and headed to the back room. In one corner were a coffee table and two oversized armchairs. Moses was sitting in one of them, his wheelchair parked next to it, and there were two steaming cups on the table.

"Come into my office," Moses said grandly.

June picked up Indigo and perched on the edge of the other armchair.

"That's no way to relax," said Moses. "Push on back."

"Push on back?"

Moses grinned and pushed back in his seat. June

gasped as the armchair tilted almost all the way horizontal and the bottom popped up like a footstool supporting his legs.

"It's a recliner," said Moses, laughing at her expression. "Don't they have those in New York?"

June shook her head.

"Well, it won't bite you. Push 'er back!" Moses said again.

June leaned back but nothing happened.

"Okay, I gotta admit I was fooling with you. Reach down next to the cushion on your right—feel that handle?"

There was a handle tucked just out of sight. Moses seemed to live in a world filled with surprise handles and levers.

"That's right—now pull the handle toward you."

June pulled back with all her strength. The chair suddenly popped back, and she found herself staring at the ceiling as if she was in a dentist chair.

"Wow!" She started giggling, and Indigo poked his head over the side—the floor looked both close and far away from this position. "How do I get back?"

"Just give a shove in the other direction," Moses said. "Show her who's boss."

June leaned forward hard, and the armchair folded right back up again. She pulled the handle—sure enough, it popped into dentist-chair position. She leaned forward into armchair position.

"Holy Saskatchewan Sunday!" She turned to Moses. "That is the most awesome chair in the world!"

"Sure is," he said. "We've got a few things out here that may surprise you yet." He reached for her mug and poured in some cream-colored liquid from a small can.

"See what you think of Postum with Carnation."

"What's Carnation?"

Moses held up the can for her to see. "Carnation evaporated milk," he said proudly. "Sweet as sugar and thickens it up a little."

He handed her the mug and she prepared

herself for the worst. Back home she had an espresso maker, and she loved to use the milk steamer to froth up some milk, then add a drop of almond or vanilla extract as a treat. She distrusted all powdered- and canned-milk products, and the one time she had tried a sip of Shirley Rosenbloom's coffee, she hadn't been able to stomach it. But Moses was giving her such a hopeful look, she closed her eyes and swallowed. It was definitely *not* coffee. It was a little weird, very sweet, and in fact . . . kind of perfect. She opened her eyes and smiled.

"Thank you," she said. "This is delicious. I never had it before."

"Two firsts!" Moses said, leaning back with his mug of Postum like an expert (he went horizontal without spilling a drop).

"Now," Moses said, "tell me about your mother."

June wondered if there was truth serum in the Postum, and by the time each of them had a second cup, she had told Moses everything: Mr. Mendax losing all her money, the last-minute flight to

South Dakota, the trouble with Aunt Bridget, and of course, the Penny Book. Moses listened without interruption, though he did raise his eyebrows a couple of times and cocked his head to the side just the way Indigo Bunting did when he was paying close attention. The only thing she didn't tell him about was the list. For some reason, that felt like a secret she was supposed to keep. After she finished there was a long pause.

"Odd thing, that Penny Book," he said at last.

"Have you ever heard of one before?" June asked. Maybe it was a midwestern thing, like Postum.

"I used to collect coins myself. Probably still have that jar somewhere. But what your mom did, writing about the day she found it and then something from the date of the penny—now, that's creative."

"Bob sure knew about it," June said darkly. "And Aunt Bridget wanted to get rid of it."

"It doesn't make sense, though," Moses said, reaching across to ruffle Indigo's ears. The pig had fallen asleep, sprawled out in the warm armchair. "Why wouldn't she want you to have it? And why would she tell you she'd tossed it in the drop box when she hadn't?"

"'Cause she hates me?" June offered. She was trying to make a joke, but Moses looked at her seriously.

"As far as I know, hate can't really breathe without its opposite," he said gently. "Some people do hate, it's true; I've seen it. But most of us just do the wrong thing sometimes. Misguided. Don't know why."

June didn't want to be rude to Moses, so she stared hard into her empty mug. "Some of those pennies are worth a lot of money," she said slowly. "My mom wrote in her penny book about finding the Big One. Maybe Aunt Bridget stole it from her and doesn't want me to find out."

"But wasn't your mother the rich one, and your aunt the poor one?" Moses asked.

June put her head back and closed her eyes, suddenly exhausted. Nothing made any sense, starting with this conversation with a strange old man in the back of a second-hand clothing shop in Red Bank, South Dakota.

The bell at the front of the store rang, and June popped forward in her recliner, shocked by the intrusion. Moses laughed and swung forward more slowly.

"First customer of the day," he said cheerfully.

A voice called out, "Moses? You here?"

"We're in the back!" Moses winked at June. "No customers yet."

June pulled Indigo onto her lap as she heard someone walk their way. For a split second she wondered if it was Aunt Bridget come looking for her, but then there he was again: Joe, the Tunafish Boy with those big blue eyes and a cowlick that stuck straight up like Indigo's tail when he was surprised. Joe looked as shocked to see June as she was to see him.

Moses waved at him. "Morning, Joe. Want a cup of Postum? This is June. She's new in town."

Joe nodded without saying anything.

"We've met," June said. "We're in the same class." Then, after a beat, "In the same detention, if you want to know the truth."

"Huh," said Moses. "Didn't know I was running a home for juvenile delinquents."

Joe smiled and June felt a little relieved. At least the boy had a sense of humor, plus he didn't smell like tuna fish today.

"Is that yours?" Joe asked, pointing at Indigo.

"Yes," June said. "Say hello, Indigo." Indigo held out a trotter, and June could tell he missed wearing his top hat out here in the country. Joe looked surprised but shook Indigo's trotter politely. "Pleased to meet you." He turned back to June. "Indigo?"

"Indigo Bunting," she said primly, tucking the pig under her arm. "And before you ask, he's a miniature pig with the name of a bird, and yes, he's housebroken."

Joe's eyes widened and June added impatiently, "We're from New York."

"Joe works here Saturdays," Moses said briskly. "Sorting and labeling, sometimes working the cash register when I'm busy. Don't see any reason why you can't work here as well."

"Me?" June was stunned. Work? June had never given a thought to working except for some vague idea that someday a fabulous job would come her way that allowed her to save the world while looking exactly like Audrey Hepburn in *Breakfast at Tiffany's*.

"Your aunt giving you an allowance?" Moses asked.

"No," June said slowly. She felt Joe looking at her and started to blush. She didn't want him to know that she came from a rich family—he'd think she was spoiled. There was an awkward pause. Maybe she *was* spoiled, June thought with horror. She had never thought of herself as spoiled, just rich. But maybe that was the same thing in South Dakota. Maybe that was the same thing everywhere!

"I pay three dollars an hour," said Moses. "Not the state minimum, but not bad for Red Bank."

"Can't do better except for lifeguarding at the

pool," said Joe. "And you have to be sixteen for that, plus it's only in summer."

"I'm not much of a swimmer," said June, feeling herself blush even harder. A spoiled rich kid. Is that what she was?

"It's settled, then," said Moses. "Joe can show you the ropes out back. I'm going to man the register."

Moses hitched himself back into the wheelchair: he locked the wheels, picked up one leg, then the other, and lifted himself into the seat using just his arms. June was impressed with how easy he made it look. She had a hard time pulling herself out of the pool just with her arms! But Moses was very strong for an old man, and once he was back in the chair, he headed into the shop and settled behind the cash register up front, turning on a large transistor radio that was tuned to a country-music station. Joe shrugged at June and led the way to the piles of black garbage bags stuffed with clothes, and cardboard boxes with kitchen discards poking out the top. Indigo closed his eyes and stretched out a little more comfortably. June glared at him and thought she might just have heard a snore, or was that a chuckle? Only Indigo could do both at the same time.

14
Don't Worry, Be Happy

It was the slowest hour of June's life. She couldn't believe that she had only earned $3.00 by the time it was over. Actually it was $2.50 once she subtracted the cost of the Dalmatian sweater. All she really wanted to do was sit down with Indigo and try to puzzle out her mother's list, but first she and Joe had to empty out the garbage bags. They threw roughly half of what was donated into a bin headed for the landfill. Who would donate dirty socks? Not to mention the unmentionables. Before they began to sort, Joe made them both put on rubberized dish-washing gloves, and she thought he was being a little ridiculous until she saw some of the things that came out of those bags.

You could tell right away if they were accept-able donations by whether or not the clothes were folded. Even though most of the donations arrived in garbage bags, some people folded neatly, and there was no question that those clothes had been washed. Other bags were crammed to bursting, and if it had been up to June, she would have thrown them directly into the landfill.

"Do we really have to look through this one?" she asked Joe after pulling out three balled-up pairs of tights.

Joe shrugged. "Once I found a brand-new leather jacket at the bottom of a bag filled with sauce packets from a Chinese restaurant."

"You're kidding!" June stopped sorting. "Where is it?"

"Hanging in my closet," Joe said with a grin. "Moses lets you buy things half price if you find something good. Sometimes he even lets you have it for free."

"No, I mean the Chinese restaurant," said June. "I didn't see one in town. I love Chinese food, and I especially love getting it to go."

Joe looked surprised. "I don't know. I guess there must be one in Sioux Falls. Never been."

"You've never had Chinese food?"

"Nope. But I've got a great leather jacket."

Joe tied up a bag of discards and tossed it behind his back into the garbage bin. He made the shot from about ten feet away. He grinned and said in a fake sportscaster's voice: "He shoots! He scores!" June pretended not to notice.

"How come you moved here?" Joe asked after a little while.

"I didn't," June said abruptly. "I was forced to come live with my aunt because of money."

Joe nodded. "My mom almost had to give me up after my dad died, because of money. Lots of people told her to put me into foster care, but she said *no way*. She's getting unemployment since she got laid off, so that's good."

June wondered what "getting unemployment" meant but thought she'd sound stupid if she asked, so she just nodded.

June felt something hard in the bag and pulled out a big plastic fish that was mounted on a piece of wood. She stared at it.

Joe clapped his hands and the fish started singing, its rubber lips moving and its tail wiggling. "Don't worry, be happy. Don't worry . . . be happy."

June shrieked and dropped it onto the table, where it kept right on singing. Joe laughed out loud, and Indigo Bunting ran over to see what all the fuss was about.

"What the— What is that thing?" June asked as the fish ended its song with a final wiggle of its rubber lips.

Joe could barely breathe, he was laughing so hard. "You've never seen one before?" He clapped his hands again just as Indigo was reaching in for a sniff, and the pig jumped back as the fish started up again: "Don't worry, be happy."

"Leaping Liberace," said June, getting closer now. "It's like—a joke thing?"

This made Joe laugh even harder. "Yeah," he said between breaths. "They used to be all over the place. Restaurants, gas stations, everybody had 'em."

The song stopped and Joe clapped again, and this time Indigo knew what to expect. He got up on his hind legs and began to do his own choreography, forearms in the air and hips swaying.

June started laughing at Joe's shocked expression. "We used to watch a lot of *American Idol*," she said apologetically. "He'll dance to anything as long as there's a bass line." There certainly was a bass line, and Indigo was clearly enjoying showing off his moves. She picked him up and put him onto the long table—he began to moonwalk.

"Your pig—*moonwalks?*" Joe was awestruck.

"He's just a big show-off." Indigo slid toward them on his knees for a big finish. "You should see him when he dances to Michael Jackson. He's out of control."

Joe clapped to start the song up again, and this time they both cracked up as Indigo began his routine with an ambitious pirouette and landed on his hindquarters with a thump.

"Working hard? Or hardly working?" asked a voice sarcastically, and there was Aunt Bridget. She stood in the doorway, and Moses was right behind her with an apologetic expression.

"Aunt Bridget!" June grabbed Indigo in the middle of his bow and took a few steps back, putting as much space as possible between them. "What are you doing here?"

"Well, after you walked out on me"—Aunt Bridget's eyes bored into her—"I figured I'd give you a little time to tire yourself out before I came to pick you up on the road—"

"I didn't *want* to get picked up!"

Aunt Bridget ignored her. "I drove back and forth a few times, but no sign of you or the critter." She nodded at Indigo. "Eventually, I figured I'd come into town myself to look for you. Agata, down at the hardware store, told me she'd seen a strange girl riding by in the passenger seat of Moses's truck." She turned to glare at Moses then back at June. "I figured out who that might be from the description: 'strange.'"

Moses started to say something but Aunt Bridget barreled on.

"And don't you ever get in a car with a stranger again! You were lucky this time but that is dangerous behavior, and you follow my rules when you are living with me! You are in a lot of trouble, Missy."

"I never wanted to live with you and my name is not Missy!" June shouted. Aunt Bridget looked like she was about to blow, and Moses held up his hands to stop them.

"It's my fault, Bridget. I should have called you when we got here," he began. "I wasn't sure where she came from at first, or that you didn't know—"

"I didn't know where this girl had gone, and apparently she didn't see fit to tell me!" Bridget interrupted, giving them both a hard look.

June took a deep breath. "I came down here to get my mother's Penny Book. What I think is strange is that it wasn't in the drop box like you said it was."

Aunt Bridget looked flustered for half a second, then recovered. "I gave it to Bob to bring down here. Same difference. Guess he hasn't gotten to it yet."

"Guess not," said June. The silence lengthened between them.

Moses looked from one to the other. "I tell you what," he said to Aunt Bridget. "I can use another hand down here with the donations, and me or Joe can drive her home when her shift's over. That way, when Bob comes down with the book, June can just—"

"No," said Aunt Bridget in a tone of voice that made even Moses look taken aback. "That book is gone. She's coming home right now."

"No, I'm not!" June said, her voice rising. "I am not coming home until—"

"Until we finish our English project," Joe interrupted. June and Aunt Bridget both stared at him.

"We have a big presentation on Monday, and June and I are supposed to do research at the library this afternoon."

Aunt Bridget opened her mouth and closed it again, just like the rubber fish. "Since when do you have a homework project that requires the library?" she asked June.

"Since you made me go to school," June shot back. "I was fine with homeschooling! Did you know that colleges accept more homeschooled kids than ever before because we work at our own pace, which means—"

"Enough!" Aunt Bridget interrupted. "That is quite enough out of you!" She looked hard at Joe. "You're Joe Pye, aren't you?"

"Yes, ma'am."

"Live with your mother out past Freeman Road?"

"Yes, ma'am."

"You and June in the same class, then?"

"Yes, ma'am. Mr. Fitzroy's English."

"Hmmph! That know-nothing." June thought it best to keep her eyes trained directly between Indigo's ears. "Very well," Aunt Bridget said. "You may go to the library for this 'project'—a royal waste of time, if I know Henry Fitzroy—but school is school. How will you get home?"

"I'll drive her," Joe said. Aunt Bridget raised her eyebrows and he continued, "I can give her a ride on the tractor. That's how I get to work and back, and it's legal on the roads. Tractor won't go more than fifteen miles an hour."

"I know how fast a tractor can drive," Aunt Bridget snapped. She sighed and looked at Moses, who gave her a small nod. "We'll talk about the job later," she said to June. "For now, you go to the library with Joe and then straight home."

June nodded without smiling, though she knew that Joe and Moses both expected her to thank her aunt. There was nothing to thank her for as far as June was concerned. Nobody had ever been in charge of June Sparrow; she was in charge of herself.

Aunt Bridget stood there expectantly until Moses finally broke in. "You go ahead and get your homework done, Joe. You can make up the hours next weekend."

"Thanks, Moses." Joe grabbed his jacket.

"I'll see you back home before supper," Aunt Bridget said to June. "No funny business or I'll know about it right quick, make no mistake about that."

"Yes, ma'am," June said, in such a perfect imitation of Joe's polite tone of voice that Aunt Bridget did a double take. She looked as if she couldn't decide if June was being rude or not.

"The tractor's out back," Joe said. June looked at Moses, who winked and nodded. This was all a game, June realized. Joe might have thought up the library idea, but all they really had to do was drive around the block, and Aunt Bridget would be gone by then. She certainly wasn't going to leave before Bob got there with the Penny Book. She grabbed Indigo Bunting and followed Joe, with Aunt Bridget watching her every move.

There really was a big green tractor with huge muddy wheels in the parking lot, though June seemed the only one surprised by it. Joe climbed up on the metal seat and held out a hand for her to grab as she clambered up to sit next to him. The seat was plenty wide, but all of a sudden it seemed to be perched very high above the ground. Indigo Bunting looked at her doubtfully.

"Are you sure this is safe?" she asked Joe. He turned the key in the ignition with one hand and held the enormous steering wheel with the other. The motor started right up and everything began to shake. June felt her teeth and her toes rattling, and Indigo pressed himself even closer to her.

"You okay?" asked Joe loudly over the engine.

Aunt Bridget was standing off to the side, looking like she was ready to trail them to the library, but her aunt appeared much less frightening from the high seat of the tractor. June felt a small rush of triumph.

"Yes!" she yelled back to Joe.

"What?" He looked over to make sure she was okay.

"Nothing!" June yelled, and despite Aunt Bridget she found herself smiling. Joe grinned back and she punched his shoulder. "Get going!" she yelled. "We've got to get to work on this project, right?"

"What?"

"Drive!"

The tractor started off with such a strong lurch, June almost fell off the back. She put one hand on the seat and the other hand on Indigo. As they pulled out of the parking lot, Aunt Bridget was still watching, and Moses was at the door of the shop, waving to her. June waved and was surprised when Aunt Bridget waved back along with Moses. Goodbye and good riddance, thought June as they pulled onto Main Street. They might not have been exactly leaving Aunt Bridget in the dust, but it was as close as she could get for now.

15
Main Street

When they got to the corner, June tapped Joe on the shoulder. "Turn around!" she yelled in his ear. "We have to go back!"

"How come?" he yelled.

"Penny Book! Bob could come down any minute!"

"Moses will keep it safe," Joe shouted. "We'd better go to the library like we said."

June started to protest, then stopped herself. First of all, it was very difficult to have a conversation while riding on a tractor, and it was awfully fun to ride. Second of all, Joe was right. Moses knew even better than Joe how important the Penny Book was to her, and the shop wasn't exactly busy. He would certainly notice if Bob came by and left it in the drop box. She could check the box again after they pretended to do whatever they were supposed to do at the library. Besides, she was curious; June Sparrow really loved libraries.

As the tractor progressed slowly down Main Street, June had another chance to check out the town. The two girls were still sitting in front of the coffee shop in their lawn chairs next to the rack of clothes. June tapped on Joe's shoulder. "Pull over!"

"Huh?"

"Pull over!"

He slowed the tractor down and pulled up to the curb. There weren't many cars parked on Main Street, so there was plenty of room.

"We're supposed to go straight to the library," Joe said, turning around on the seat. June slid down to the sidewalk with Indigo.

"This will only take a second," she said. "I want to shop!"

June walked over to the girls, who suddenly seemed very interested in the magazines on their laps—until they saw Indigo peeking his head out of June's arms.

"Oh, he is so *cute*!" one of the girls said. "What *is* he?"

June smiled and held Indigo out to show them.

"He's a pig?" the other girl said. "A tiny pig!"

"A miniature pig," June said proudly. "You want to hold him?"

"Will he let us?" asked the first girl.

"Of course!" June handed off a warm and wriggling Indigo Bunting.

Indigo loved meeting new people, and he licked the girl right on the tip of her nose as she held him in her arms.

"My name is June," June said, grateful to Indigo for breaking the ice.

"You're new, right? I'm Keisha and this is my sister, Aliyah," said the girl holding Indigo.

"We're twins, but not identical," Aliyah said. "Seems obvious, but you wouldn't believe how many people ask us that. Hi, Joe." June turned to see that Joe had just walked up.

"How's it going?" Joe's face had gone beet red.

"Can you believe how cute he is?" Luckily, Aliyah was talking about Indigo, not Joe. "My turn," she said, and Keisha reluctantly handed him over. Aliyah promptly sat down with Indigo on her lap and started making high-pitched cooing noises, which Indigo responded to graciously, though June knew he didn't like it when people spoke baby talk to him just because he was little.

June started to flip through the clothing racks. There were lots of matching little-girl dresses that looked like they might have come from the sisters' own closets.

"Everything is fifty cents to five dollars," Keisha said.

"Or best offer," Aliyah said, looking up from Indigo, whose curly tail was going a mile a minute, despite the baby talk.

"*You* do best offer," Keisha said, rolling her eyes at her sister. "I try to stick to the price since we donate it all to charity." She smiled at Joe. "Your mom bought some great stuff last Saturday. Maybe you want to get her something?"

"We have to be at the library," Joe mumbled, looking anywhere but at her. "School report."

June started to protest, but then she remembered that Aunt Bridget seemed to have eyes in the back of her head. She wished that she could buy something, just to be friendly, but then she remembered that she still had to work off the Dalmatian sweater she was wearing. She couldn't afford to go into the coffee shop either, she realized. It was easy to forget that life without cash in her pockets was very, very different.

"Thanks anyway," June said, after a beat.

"Nice to meet you," said Aliyah, handing back Indigo. "He's the cutest little pig I ever saw."

"Thank you," said June. "And good luck with the sidewalk sale." The girls waved and Indigo waved back with one of his little trotters, which sent them into paroxysms of giggles.

"They're nice," June said as she clambered up next to Joe on the tractor.

"Yep." Joe was still blushing, though the red had faded a tiny bit. He looked over his shoulder and paused. "You might as well know it—I don't really have a lot of friends at school. I don't like sports, and all the boys play sports. Plus we moved here after my dad left, so . . ." Joe's voice trailed off and he looked away.

"I don't have a dad either," June said, wishing she could think of something more encouraging to say. "Or a mom. It's just me and Indigo, which is fine by me, but nobody here seems to understand pigs as pets. I'll bet I've got the weirdest family in town."

Joe brightened a bit and turned back to take the wheel. "I don't think you're weird," he said. "And pigs as pets are fine by me."

Joe turned the ignition and they started off again down Main Street, the tractor's engine breaking the quiet of the afternoon. There were three pickup trucks parked in front of the hardware store, and one of them had a horse trailer attached. A long brown tail peeked out, swishing back and forth. The woman who had been sweeping the sidewalk earlier was leaning in the driver's-side window, chatting with the driver. She looked up and waved as Joe drove by, and he lifted a couple of fingers off the wheel and nodded in acknowledgment. June thought it was kind of sweet the way people waved to each other in Red Bank, and she wished that she could run her hands down that beautiful horse tail, but she didn't dare ask Joe to stop for a second time.

They passed a closed-up video store and a beauty parlor June hadn't noticed before: Goldie's Goldilocks. There were two women staring out the window at them with big curlers in their hair— maybe one of them was Goldie. They must have a sense of humor, thought June, to name the shop Goldie's Goldilocks, and she did the queen wave from the back of the tractor with her fingers cupped together. She had seen the queen of England do this on television. Both women pulled back from the

how much Indigo had enjoyed the tractor ride that he wasn't offended by this remark. Joe jumped off and June handed him Indigo, then climbed down after him. Joe gave one of the tractor's enormous wheels an affectionate pat, as if he was leaving his horse tied to a hitching rail, and led the way to the front door of the library.

16
Numismatics

The library was actually inside a trailer, June realized as she got closer, with the outside painted brown to make it look like wood. She wondered if it was the kind of trailer that had wheels so it could be a mobile library. There were mobile book trailers parked along the edge of Central Park, near the zoo, and June used to love to browse these mini bookstores. It was the perfect way to end a day in the park with Indigo. But this was a real library, so June tried to hide Indigo so that he wouldn't be seen. She and Joe pulled open the front door, which had a small brass bell on a string.

The library looked bigger once you were inside. The librarian was the only person there, sitting behind a desk at one end of the long room. Two study carrels with computers took up the center of the trailer, and the walls were all bookshelves. At the opposite end was the children's corner, with picture books displayed on low shelves, wooden puzzles, and a comfy-looking armchair for reading.

"Hello, Miss Flores," Joe said.

"Hello, Joe." Miss Flores looked just the way a librarian was supposed to look—the nice kind of librarian, that is. She was wearing a rose-colored cardigan and had her dark hair pulled up in a bun. Her glasses were tortoiseshell, and they somehow made her look prettier as well as smarter.

"I'm June Sparrow," June said, walking over to the desk. "I've just moved here and would like to apply for a library card, please."

"Certainly," Miss Flores said. "All we need is your address."

June struggled for a moment to remember the name of Aunt Bridget's road. She looked at Joe. "She's over with Miss Andersen, on Phoenicia Road," he said.

"I'm afraid I don't know the street number." June looked down. "I only just moved here."

Miss Flores nodded. "No problem. You can start using the library right away. Joe comes all the time, don't you, Joe?" Joe blushed and didn't say anything. June wondered why he would be embarrassed about using the library, but Miss Flores kept talking. "Joe can show you how to use the online catalog. We can also order books from other libraries if you need them. Our collection is a bit limited, because of space." She gave a small sigh. "On the other hand, Sioux Falls doesn't mind shipping books over to us, though it may take a few days."

June decided not to say that she was already familiar with how to use the online catalog at the New York Public Library, since Miss Flores and Joe both looked so pleased at having a new person to show around. Joe took her to one of the study carrels, pulled up a second chair, and turned on the computer.

"I just started working for the school newspaper," he said. "So I come over here a lot to do my research."

"Research?"

"When you're a reporter, you'd better have your facts straight."

"Wow!" June was impressed. "You're kind of like Clark Kent and Superman."

Joe gave her a shy smile. "Without the Superman part."

"No! Really, Joe!" Indigo pushed his face up out of her jacket and looked from one to the other, trying to find out what all the excitement was about. June pushed him back down so Miss Flores wouldn't see him and spoke in a whisper. "You seem like just a regular kid, but *really* you're a reporter!"

Joe blushed hard. "I'd love to be a *real* reporter someday."

"Why not?" June said. "Let's pretend this is

your first assignment! We can look up pennies, and maybe we can figure out which is the Big One that Aunt Bridget stole from my mom."

"Whaaat?" asked Joe. So while June Googled "rare pennies worth a lot of money," she explained to him what had happened the night before, and that morning, and why the Penny Book was so important not just because of her mom, but because of the missing penny itself.

"Really?" Joe said when she was done. "You think your mom had a penny that could make you rich?"

"Sssh!" June said, looking at Miss Flores, who was putting up a new poster on the door and trying not to listen. "I don't want anyone to know about this. Except Moses, and now you, I guess. But you can't tell anyone—really, you can't. Pretend you're breaking a big news story and you can't tell anyone until it's on the front page."

"Okay," Joe said seriously. "But why do you think your aunt stole it?"

"It's missing, isn't it?" asked June. "Besides,

you saw how weird she was acting about my not getting the Penny Book."

"Yeah," Joe said. "That was weird, considering it's your mom and all. But your aunt isn't rich, and if she did steal the Big One, then how come—"

"That's exactly what Moses said." June sighed. "Okay, maybe she didn't steal it. Or maybe she stole it and still has the money hidden somewhere. Maybe she's still living off the money since she only works on the farm."

"Lots of people around here only work on the farm," said Joe doubtfully.

"Well, maybe my mom took it with her. I don't know! But Aunt Bridget must know *something* since she didn't want me to keep looking at the Penny Book." June suddenly broke off, staring at the screen. "Hey! Numismatics! That's the name of my parents' company! I never knew what it meant—I figured it was some old family name and never bothered to look it up. 'The study or collecting of coins, metals, and the like.' It says that a coin collector is called a numismatologist. Then there's 'numismatical' and 'numismatology'—"

"How come your parents' company was called that?" Joe interrupted.

"I don't know," June said slowly. "They did have a valuable coin collection, but they collected lots of things. Tin soldiers, old toys, seventy-eight records . . . my apartment was full of really cool stuff."

"What kind of a company was it?" Joe asked.

"Mom and Dad invented Sticky Glue," she said. "You know, that stuff they put onto regular paper to turn it into a Post-it note?"

Joe might be an investigative reporter, but he was clearly not a stationery nerd.

"Look." June nodded toward Miss Flores. The librarian was rubbing what looked like a glue stick across the back of the poster and sticking it to the door.

"Sticky Glue," June said matter-of-factly. "Everybody uses it. It was bad news for Post-it notes but good news for everybody else. You can use it to stick any piece of paper onto the wall, or even a computer screen. Better than glue because it doesn't leave a mark when you move it around. See?"

"Holy moly," Joe said, watching Miss Flores move the poster a few inches higher. It stuck to the door like magic. "I know that stuff. So you're, like—the Sticky Glue heiress?"

"I *was*," said June. "The company had to be sold, right down to the last Sticky Glue stick." She turned to Joe with a weary smile. "Sad to say, I'm no longer an heiress to anything." She looked back at Miss Flores, who was happily sliding Sticky Glue across an index card and sticking it on the top of her computer. "Good invention though, huh?"

"*Really* good." Joe stared at Miss Flores and then back at June.

June waved her hand in front of him. "It's over now, remember? I'm broke, stuck in South Dakota—no offense—and my aunt hates my guts. So let's get back to work."

She turned back to the computer screen and started trolling through sites about valuable pennies. "The Big One . . . the Big One . . ." There were many charts of pennies shown by year and current value, but none of them were labeled "the Big One."

"Wow, some of these are really worth something," Joe said. "Look at this one: four dollars and sixty-five cents!"

"That's not that much," said June, still skimming.

"Compared to the original value, though, if you do the math—"

"Wait! Wait! Look at this—from the U.S. Mint site," June said. "The 1943 penny, struck in copper."

They both leaned in and read together:

According to the American Numismatic Association, the 1943 copper-alloy cent is one of the most idealized and potentially sought-after items in American numismatics.

"That's a great name for a band," said June. "The Numismatics."

Joe kept reading:

Nearly all circulating pennies at that time were struck in zinc-coated steel because copper and nickel were needed for the Allied war effort. 40 1943 copper-alloy cents are known to remain in existence. Coin experts speculate that they were struck by accident when copper-alloy 1-cent blanks remained in the press hopper when production began on the new steel pennies. A 1943 copper cent was first offered for sale in 1958, bringing more than $40,000. The highest amount paid for a 1943 copper cent was $82,500 in 1996. More recently one was auctioned for more than $1,000,000."

Joe and June stared at each other.

"A million dollars," whispered June.

"But we don't know if that's the one your mom was writing about," Joe whispered back.

"Listen to this!" June was still reading down the page at lightning speed.

The easiest way to determine if a 1943 cent is made of copper is to use a magnet. If it sticks to the magnet, it is not copper. If it does not stick, the coin might be made of copper and should be authenticated by an expert.

"This is it!" June said, jumping up. "I know this is the Big One, Joe. I just know it!"

Indigo squealed. Miss Flores looked up, even though there was nobody else in the library, and put a warning finger to her lips. June hoped she hadn't heard Indigo. "Sorry!" June whispered loudly, then more quietly to Joe. "It all makes sense. My mom and Bob were looking for the Big One, and this is the Biggest One there is! See, it says right there: 'one of the most idealized and potentially sought-after items in American numismatics.' *That's* the Big One."

Joe looked at June, then back at the screen.

"I'll tell you one thing," he said slowly. "We'd better get a magnet."

"A magnet?"

Joe pointed at the screen. "If it's the Big One, it

won't stick to a magnet. That's how we'll know for sure."

June suddenly sat down.

Find metal that won't stick to a magnet

"Is there a bathroom here?" she asked a little shakily. Joe pointed toward the end of the library, and June walked there in a daze. She locked the rickety door behind her and pulled out her mother's list. Indigo popped his head out so that he could look over her shoulder, and there it was:

Travel inside a beehive

and

Find metal that won't stick to a magnet

"It's like Mom knew I would be here, looking for the Big One, meeting Moses and riding in his truck, but how could any of that be possible?" she said to Indigo, who shook his head, looking as confused as she was.

"This whole list is a riddle," she said. A riddle she was supposed solve with her mother. June quickly scanned what was left on the list:

Climb a ladder to the top of the world
Hug my oldest friend
Eat ice cream for breakfast
Take a ride on the La-Z-Boy express
Let gonebyes go bye-bye

Then there were those weird initials and numbers at the top:

J.S. 2 R.B. 4 B.D.

June wished that her mother was right here, right now, to let her know what all this meant. She looked at Indigo and sighed. June Sparrow was good at lots of things. Solving riddles was not one of them.

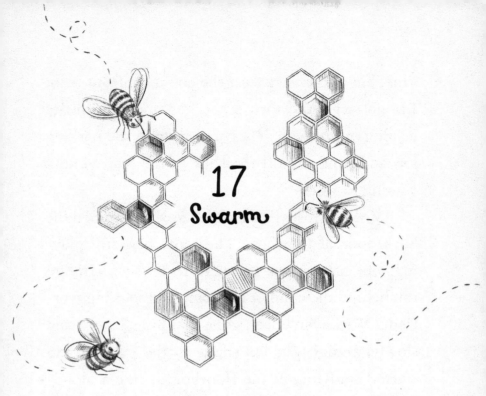

17
Swarm

They said good-bye to Miss Flores, who seemed slightly disappointed that they had only used the computer instead of taking out a book, but June assured her that she would be back soon. They headed back to the This 'n' That shop, and though June still loved riding the tractor and Joe had the pedal to the metal, she wished it went faster than fifteen miles per hour. The Penny Book might be in the drop box right now! Somehow she felt certain that the Penny Book would help her to find the Big

One, but at the very least she could confront Aunt Bridget with the torn-out pages and the entries leading up to them. They pulled up in the parking lot, and June slid off the back of the seat without waiting for Joe.

"Moses! Moses!" she called as she slammed the back door of the shop. The radio was still playing, but Moses was nowhere to be seen. Indigo ran behind the counter and came out looking worried. "We haven't been gone that long," June said slowly. Indigo put his snout to the ground and started snuffling at the floorboards like a bloodhound. "Oh really, Indigo." June rolled her eyes. "I'm sure he's just gone out for a cup of coffee or something." Indigo picked up his head and gave her a look.

Ever since they had watched a cooking show about the truffle-hunting pigs of France, who sniff out the rarest and most expensive mushrooms in the world, Indigo took every opportunity to act like a truffle hunter. He snorted his way to the back room. Moses wasn't in his recliner, but June heard voices from a room just beyond the sorting room. Indigo pushed forward triumphantly with June right behind him. It was a small, glass-enclosed porch, and Moses was in his wheelchair in front of a wooden loom.

Joe must have gone directly there, and Indigo was running excitedly from one to the other, wagging his curly tail and acting as if it had been years since he had seen either one of them.

"Were you worried about me, little guy?" Moses reached down to scratch between his ears.

Indigo ran back to June, filled with pride, and June picked him up for a hug and whispered "Truffle hunter" into his little pink ear.

Moses was sitting at the loom, pushing a piece of wood with some brightly colored material across a set of threads—back and forth, back and forth. There was an electric hum, and Indigo sniffed at two broad foot pedals below the whole contraption. They were hooked up to a small engine that kept them going back and forth automatically, like keys on a player piano.

"You know how to weave?" June asked.

"It's pretty easy once you get the hang of it," Moses said, staying focused on the weave in front of him. "Things go well at the library?"

June gave Joe a quick look. She didn't want him to tell anyone, even Moses, about how much the Big One might be worth. "Great," she said. "We found everything we needed."

She walked over to stand next to Moses, who nodded toward the loom while his hands kept moving. "I've got a couple of side businesses. There's the bees, of course, to sell honey and make beeswax products in the winter. This here is for making rag rugs, but all the profits go to charity."

"What's a rag rug?" asked June. The weaving on the loom in front of Moses was a blend of yellow, red, and orange, and each stripe was slightly different. There were hints of plaid patterns if you looked closely, and knobbly places where the material was soft and bunchy like a bath towel.

"People used to make rag rugs by hand," Moses said. "But the church committee invested in a loom for the shop, since it's for charity. The congregation decides where to donate. Different place every year. There's the pile of rugs that are done." Moses nodded toward a plastic bin. "Believe it or not, I've got commissions!"

June opened the bin and pulled out the top one. It was about twice as big as a bath mat, with fringes on both ends. The materials were different types, but the way the colors went together was just right. She had never seen a rag rug before and immediately decided that this was her favorite kind of rug in the world.

"These are beautiful, Moses!" She pulled out one after the other. "How do you choose what material to use?"

"That depends on what comes in," he said cheerfully.

"What comes in where?"

"Here."

June looked at Joe.

"Moses makes the rugs from what comes into the shop," Joe said.

"Right now I'm working with Mrs. Hanover's bathrobe," Moses said. "She was a lovely lady. Passed in August. Age ninety-three."

June dropped the rug she was holding. "You mean the material for the rugs comes from dead people?"

"Sometimes," Moses said. "After someone passes, a lot of their things come to the shop. If something catches my eye that looks like good rug material, we set it aside."

"I cut the material into strips for the rugs," Joe said. "I've done a little weaving, not too much."

"You're on your way," Moses said. "You'll have one for your mom by Christmas."

Mom. Christmas. "Wait! Moses, has my aunt's friend Bob come in yet? With the Penny Book?"

Moses and Joe exchanged looks. "No, I'm afraid not." Moses stopped the loom to look at her. "But maybe later today . . ."

"Can we check the drop box?"

"I would have heard if anyone pulled up—"

"But you might not have, right? With the radio

playing and working the loom. You might not have heard—"

"I've got a bell on the front door, June," Moses said gently. "And the porch here faces out back, so if anybody drops something off—"

"Please, Moses. Please give me the key so I can go check. Please?"

There was a pause.

"Okay, Joe, take her out there," Moses said. "After that, I guess you'd better run her home like we promised."

Joe led the way to the parking lot, picking up Moses's large key ring, which was sitting on the donations table. He and June went out the back door, and once they were out of earshot June said to Joe, "Don't you think it's kind of weird to use clothes from dead people to make the rugs? I mean, they're like, zombie rugs."

"I don't know." Joe shrugged. "I don't think it's weird to wear clothes from the shop, do you?"

"No . . ."

"And maybe, I don't know. Maybe it's kind of

nice that someone like Mrs. Hanover could give one last time to charity. That's one reason Moses gets so many commissions: everyone knows it's for a good cause."

June realized that, other than giving money to people on the street when she had spare change, she had never really thought about giving to charity. Mr. Mendax handled all that for her. She had never even asked which charities her parents' donations went to every year, and now she didn't have anything to give. Joe crouched down and fitted the key to the back of the drop box. When I track down the Big One, June thought, and move back to New York, I can give a ton to charity. I'll commission forty rag rugs for Christmas.

The metal door swung open with a creak, but the box was empty. June put her hand inside to feel around, even though she knew it was pointless.

"Sorry," Joe said. "It's still kinda early—"

Just then they heard a loud buzzing sound and stared at each other. The air around them was suddenly filled with bees. They ran toward the shop.

"Moses!" Joe yelled.

Moses was already on his way, wheeling himself down the ramp and pulling a helmet with a veil attached over his head. "They're swarming!" He pointed to a low-hanging tree branch near the back of his truck. There was a large black shape that looked like some kind of material draped over the branch until you looked closely—and realized it was moving. The black cloud was a swarm of honeybees.

"Get me one of those plastic bins, Joe!" Moses went straight to the back of the pickup, squinting at the tree limb just overhead. Joe ran inside the shop, and June and Indigo shrank back in the doorway. Some of the bees were circling in a cloud over the parking lot, but more and more of them were gathering on the tree limb.

"Moses! Be careful!" June yelled. Moses had on his helmet and veil, but he was right in the midst of them.

"Don't worry," he called. "They're really gentle. Floyd's just a little upset right now."

June grabbed Indigo and debated going inside until it was all over, but she couldn't help wanting to see what was going to happen. Joe came tearing out of the shop, carrying a big plastic bin with a lid on top. June saw him hesitate, but then he went right up to the back of the truck and handed the bin to Moses, who placed it on his lap.

"Now step away," Moses said, and Joe ran back to stand with June and Indigo. June held her breath as Moses positioned his wheelchair right under the bee cloud, then reached up and gave the branch a hard jerk. About half of the buzzing black cone tumbled into the plastic bin. Moses flipped the lid closed and started to back away from the swarm. The other bees were buzzing furiously around him.

"Oh my gosh," June breathed. "He's going to get stung so badly—"

"Watch," said Joe. "Just watch."

Moses went over to the hive on the side of the truck, opened the top, and emptied the bin right into it. June gasped and pulled back as another cloud of bees rose up, but Moses stayed right in the middle of them.

"He doesn't even brush them off," whispered Joe. "See? Even when they're mad, they don't sting Moses."

Moses went back to the tree limb with the empty bin and jerked the branch again. This time almost the entire black cloud came tumbling in, and he closed the lid and slowly—maddeningly slowly, as far as June was concerned—Moses made his way back for a second time and reached up to remove the board that rested on top of the hive. But he must have reached a little too far, because all of a sudden Moses lost his balance and fell right out of his wheelchair onto the ground. The bin flew open, the lid skittered across the parking lot, and bees swirled all around Moses, who sprawled onto the pavement.

June and Joe both ran toward him. There were bees everywhere, and they couldn't stop to swat at them or get the wheelchair. Joe grabbed Moses under the shoulders; June hooked her arms under his knees. He was heavier than he looked. She and

Joe pulled with all their might toward the back door. The enraged bees were following, and even once June and Joe got Moses away from the truck, the bees still came after them.

"Inside!" yelled Joe, and they half carried, half dragged Moses up the ramp.

"Don't hurt them!" Moses murmured as Joe pulled him through the door and June slammed it shut. The fastest bees followed them inside, and Joe slapped at them as June knelt down next to Moses.

"Are you okay?"

Moses pushed the hat and veil off the top of his head. He pushed himself up to a seated postion, patted up and down his legs, and looked at them.

"I'm fine," he said. "A little shaken up. But I'll be just fine." He took a deep breath. "Too bad I lost half the hive."

June stared at him in disbelief. She wanted to shake him for caring more about the bees than himself. Moses put out his arms and June collapsed into them, not knowing whether she was laughing or crying.

Fifteen minutes later, Moses was back in his wheelchair (Joe had bravely gone back out to grab it) and June and Joe were both lying back in the recliners with cold cans of soda pop and slices of raw onion taped over their beestings. She had five stings and Joe had four. Moses had none, and said that raw onion was the best cure in the world for beestings. He always kept a few onions and a roll of adhesive tape handy. Strangely enough, June's stings started to subside as soon as Moses taped on the onion slice.

Indigo was the most dramatic of the three: he had wisely (if dishonorably) run inside when Moses fell down, then watched the rest of the drama unfold from the glassed-in porch. But just when things were settling down, one last angry bee had flown right up and stung him on the eyelid. Now he had one eye taped shut and was cradled in June's arms, feeling extremely sorry for himself. He looked like a pirate and smelled like onion.

"Best thing for beestings is a ride on the La-Z-Boy express," Moses said as he pulled up his wheelchair between the two recliners.

June popped up.

"What did you say?"

"Best thing for beestings—"

"No, no, after that!"

"The La-Z-Boy express?"

"Yes! What is that, Moses? You've got to tell me!"

Moses smiled at her excitement and patted one of the armchairs. "This here is the La-Z-Boy express. These recliners are also called La-Z-Boys. Didn't you know that?"

June stared at him.

The La-Z-Boy express.

"No. No, you didn't tell me," she said slowly.

"Great name for it," Joe said with his eyes closed. "Really takes the sting off."

18
Make a List and Check It Twice

Moses decided to close up shop early and told Joe to give June a ride home so she wouldn't be late for Aunt Bridget. June and Indigo climbed up onto the tractor, and Joe started the slow ride home. Again they rode down Main Street, and again the women in the beauty shop watched them ride by, though this time June didn't have the heart to wave. After all, she and Indigo had six beestings between them, and she couldn't say a word about the list, which was all she was really thinking about. The beehive.

The La-Z-Boy. And most of all: find metal that won't stick to a magnet. Maybe her mother's list was leading her to the Big One. But how could that be? Why had she written that list in the first place? If only June could get the Penny Book back, it might explain everything.

The sky was overcast, and the horizon was one long smudge of charcoal. It was nearly October and the temperature had dropped abruptly since midday. She wondered what winter in South Dakota was like, and all she could imagine was what she had read in *Little Town on the Prairie*, which might not be the best source since everything in that book took place about a hundred and fifty years ago.

Indigo was tucked inside the Dalmatian sweater, with his little pink snout sticking out and twitching when they rode past a particularly pungent barn. Some of the cornstalks beside the road were starting to turn brown, and June thought they looked strangely familiar, though she couldn't imagine why. Then it hit her: these were the very same kind of cornstalks that the grocery stores in New York would stack in bundles next to the pumpkins. She had seen them on the steps of brownstone buildings around Halloween and Thanksgiving. She had never really known what they were before! They were just old, dried-up cornstalks tied together in a bundle. She always thought they were some fancy dried grass that people used for decoration!

She laughed out loud, and Joe yelled over his shoulder, "What?"

June waved her hand in the air. "Tell you later!"

But she wasn't actually sure she would. Indigo stuck his head out and gave her a wink with his one good eye.

When June woke up the next morning, she had to admit it was kind of nice to see the sun streaming in the window onto her mother's Indian-print bedspread with the smell of coffee drifting up from the kitchen. She yawned, stretched, and looked around for Indigo. Her door was slightly ajar, so he must be up and out already. She wondered why Aunt

Bridget hadn't woken her up, and then she realized this was Sunday.

June wandered downstairs in her mother's pajamas. Aunt Bridget was in the kitchen, reading the Sunday paper and making waffles. The waffle iron was set up within reach so that she didn't have to take her eyes from the paper as she ladled in the waffle batter. "Good morning," she said gruffly. "Help yourself."

June felt like she could eat three breakfasts, though she had eaten a perfectly good supper of chicken and biscuits after she came home last night. She and Aunt Bridget had both been too tired to revisit their argument from the afternoon, and she hoped that the beestings seemed like enough of a punishment. June decided not to mention the Penny Book, and to keep up her investigations on her own. Moses would keep an eye on the drop box, and she had pored over the list again last night before finally tucking it under her pillow and hoping everything would come clear to her in the morning. No such luck. Even Indigo didn't have any ideas, though she read it out loud to him three times in a row while coloring his eye patch black at his insistence. (If he was going to look like a pirate, he thought that he might as well go all the way.) But she was hungry, and Aunt Bridget clearly had a Sunday-morning routine. June wondered if this extra-big breakfast was for her benefit or if her aunt did it like this every weekend: waffles, bacon (at least Aunt Bridget didn't seem to be thinking about Indigo that way anymore), canned blueberries from a Mason jar, and best of all, warmed-up maple syrup in its own little brown pitcher. Breakfast is brain food, June reminded herself, and piled her plate high (minus the bacon). Indigo was back in his snoozing spot in front of the heater in the living room, no doubt sleeping off his own farmhouse breakfast. Aunt Bridget handed June a section of the paper.

June was grateful that her aunt was not a morning talker. She couldn't stand morning talkers, and she immediately flipped to the classified section. Lots of yard sales, used tools, and farm equipment, and quite a few notices for firewood and brush hogging.

looked out the kitchen window at a small yellow bird that was having its breakfast at the bird feeder. "I go twice a year," she said. "Christmas Eve and Easter Sunday. How does that sound?"

"Great!" said June. She was more amazed that her opinion had been sought than that Aunt Bridget didn't go to church every Sunday.

"I donate, of course," Aunt Bridget said hastily. "Give to the annual charity drive, and I always go to church suppers when it's for a special cause."

June nodded vigorously.

"Our family's never been big church people," Aunt Bridget said in a confidential tone, looking at June over the top of the newspaper. "But we always give what we can."

She could tell Aunt Bridget was relieved that she wouldn't have to go to church, and June silently repeated the words: *Our family's never been big church people, but we always give what we can. . . . Our family*. It suddenly felt very important to be a member of "our family."

"Time for dessert," Aunt Bridget announced.

June was shocked. Dessert with breakfast was something she had never thought of before, though of course she was a huge fan of dessert.

Aunt Bridget walked over to the counter, where there was about half an apple pie sitting out from last night. She cut two hefty slices, then walked over to the freezer, pulled out a large carton of vanilla ice cream, and plopped a scoop on top of each slice.

Aunt Bridget dug right in, but June stared at her plate without picking up her fork.

Ice cream for breakfast.

"Don't like ice cream?" Aunt Bridget asked after a few moments.

"No," June said. "I mean yes. I like ice cream."

Her aunt looked at her. "You seemed to like that pie just fine last night."

"I love the pie!" June said, and forced herself to take a bite, but her stomach seemed to have closed up. Now there were three things on the list that she had done without even meaning to. This was getting spooky.

"Do you . . . do you always have ice cream for

breakfast?" she asked after swallowing a mouthful (which was delicious).

"Only on birthdays," Aunt Bridget said matter-of-factly.

"Is it your birthday, Aunt Bridget?" June was suddenly filled with guilt. But how could she have known?

"Nope." Aunt Bridget took another huge mouthful. "But as I recall you were born on September twenty-third, at three forty-seven in the morning."

June put her fork down and stared.

"That was last Thursday. So this is your belated birthday breakfast. I seem to be out of birthday candles, but I figured ice cream and pie would do just fine."

June stared down at her plate. So this had been her mother's birthday tradition all these years. Her mother's and Aunt Bridget's. *Our family.*

If she closed her eyes, just maybe she could remember a birthday party with her parents. She had looked through the family albums, and she knew that she'd had cake and ice cream and blown out candles. But she had only been three when her parents died, and now she was twelve. She didn't know if she was remembering the photo album or her actual birthday party. She opened her eyes and saw Aunt Bridget looking at her across the kitchen table. Just for a moment it looked like her aunt's eyes might be a little moist.

"Time to do the chores." Aunt Bridget pushed back her chair and was out the door to the barn before June could be sure of anything.

19
Bob's Pantry

September inevitably turned to October, and as the weeks went by and the weather got colder, June got accustomed to wearing more and more layers of clothing. She worked every weekend at the This 'n' That shop, so there was plenty of opportunity for her to build her wardrobe, and she checked the drop box every weekend for the Penny Book. Moses was under strict orders to grab it if he saw it during the week, but so far it had simply disappeared. June was afraid to bring it up to Aunt Bridget, hoping that her aunt assumed it had gone from Red Bank to some big collection place in Sioux Falls, and then on to a landfill. She hadn't seen Bob Burgess since that morning at the barn, and she didn't want to mention him to Aunt Bridget either, in case he reminded her of the Penny Book.

School was boring, but at least it was easy, and June figured out how to stay out of Mr. Fitzroy's way and avoid detention. It was true that Joe was considered an oddball, partly because he didn't play sports and partly because he clammed up around nearly everyone. As the weeks went by, June and Joe drifted to the same table at lunch. Joe didn't mind if June propped her library book up against a pile of textbooks to read while she was eating, too lost in her book to have a conversation. He also didn't ask her to join anything, the way some of the girls had when she first arrived.

June knew she had probably made a bad impression by politely refusing all invitations to join school clubs and teams. It turned out that Aliyah and Keisha were in her class, so they sat next to each other sometimes. But June saw this entire episode of her life as temporary and didn't want to get too involved. Did prisoners cast into dungeons join the glee club? She thought not.

Then came the Halloween dance. It was being held to benefit the PTA, but Aunt Bridget didn't volunteer to decorate, bake, or clean up. She told June that she was too busy for such foolishness, mailed a check to the PTA, and showed June where the cupcake pans were.

June was not so lucky. Even if you weren't going to the dance, the rule was that you still had to participate in decorating. The class parents had the misguided notion that it would be so much fun to decorate that any students who had thought they didn't want to go to the dance would change their minds after spending the afternoon with black and orange crepe paper. When they were finally finished, the cages around the gym lights were dutifully covered with green construction paper, and jointed paper skeletons hung glumly on the walls.

As everyone was heading out, June got a note

from the office that her aunt's car was broken down and she needed to get a ride home, because the school bus had left at the usual time with the younger kids. June read the note twice. There was nobody she could ask for a ride. None of the parents were friends with Aunt Bridget, and except for Keisha and Aliyah, none of the girls had made friends with her. She knew this was partly her own fault but still wished she could've brought Indigo to school; everybody liked Indigo. June walked out to the parking lot, hoping to see Joe, but he had gotten out of decorating because the school newspaper was supposed to come out the next day, and he had to stay late to "put the paper to bed," as he told her at lunch. June wasn't sure how long it took to put a newspaper to bed, but she didn't see Joe's tractor anywhere and figured he had already left. It was a gray, windy day, and it was going to be a long walk home.

June started walking along the highway, wishing her backpack wasn't so heavy. The sky was one big gray cloud, and most of the trees had lost their leaves, so there was nothing to break the wind. She figured it would take about an hour, but with any luck it would still be light out when she got home. She couldn't wait to see Indigo, who was indignant that miniature pigs weren't allowed to attend the Halloween dance even if they wore an opera cape and had fabulous moves. June and Indigo had always loved dressing up for Halloween, and she would have gone to the dance if Indigo had been allowed to come—but she didn't want to leave him home alone on one of his favorite holidays.

After about half a mile (or ten blocks, as June estimated it), she heard a low rumble behind her. The rumble got louder and it sounded as if someone was driving on the shoulder of the road right behind her. It was Joe on his tractor, driving on the side of the road so that cars could pass him. He was wearing a matching red cap and scarf, both of which were so lumpy, she knew they had been knit by his mother. As soon as the weather turned cold, Joe had started showing up at school wearing brightly colored homemade sweaters, which didn't exactly help his reputation. Joe looked gangly and ridiculous with his red scarf trailing behind him on the big tractor, and she had never been so glad to see him. He pulled over with a toothy smile and pulled her up onto the seat behind him without waiting for her explanation.

They trundled along companionably, though it was still going to take quite a while to get to Aunt Bridget's house. The engine was too loud for much talking, but June leaned forward at one point and asked, "Is it far for you to get home?"

Joe shook his head. "I'm out past you," he yelled, and June wondered how long it took him to drive anywhere on the tractor. On the other hand, it was awfully nice to go only slightly faster than a bicycle so that you could really see everything. They passed a green sign that said "Solid Waste/ Recycling Center One Mile," and Joe yelled, "That's the dump! Moses lives there, just a little ways down from your aunt's place."

June made a mental note of the sign. She definitely wanted to see the dump and knew that Moses would be happy to show her around. The farm they were passing now had a newly painted red barn with a gleaming metal roof behind a white board fence. It was the neatest farm they had passed so far.

"That's the Burgess place!" Joe yelled, pointing. "Looks like Bob's not home!"

June grabbed him by the shoulders. "Bob! That's Bob's place?"

"Yep. You're almost home," he called back to her.

"Wait!" yelled June. "Turn in here!"

"What?"

"Turn in! Stop!" she yelled, digging her fingers into his shoulders.

Joe slowed down and turned to look at her. "He's not home, June. There's no car in the drive."

"Perfect!"

"What do you mean?"

"I have to look for my Penny Book!"

He stopped the tractor and it tilted into the ditch that ran along the side of the road.

Joe looked at her very seriously. "We can't go

there when he's not home."

"Why not?" said June. "We're not going to steal anything; we're going to just take a look around and if I see *what's mine*, I'll take it back."

"I don't know. . . ." Joe looked extremely doubtful. He glanced from the farmhouse to the driveway and back at the house. "He's not home, June."

"That's the point!" June said, jumping down off the back of the tractor. "I may never get another chance like this!"

"I don't know," Joe said again.

"You don't have to know," June said impatiently. "I'll go and you can head home." June started across the road. "Thanks for the ride, but you don't have to wait for me," she said airily.

"But June—"

"I can walk from here. See you in school!" She turned and smiled at him. She didn't want Joe to know how much she wished he would come with her. Maybe Bob had left the Penny Book in a box on the back porch, June thought as she approached the house. She could just grab it and go. Everything was in such perfect order, she was scared that Bob would notice if she flattened a blade of grass with her sneakers. The front porch had two rockers on it, but it looked like nobody sat there very often. There was a doormat with "WELCOME" printed across it, but June decided to skirt the front door and go around the side to the kitchen. The front door was visible from the road.

She walked around to the back steps. This looked like the entrance to the house that was actually used. A pair of enormous rubber boots was on the top step, and there was a small faucet sticking out of the house that looked like it was used to wash the mud off. No wonder everything is so clean, thought June. Imagine a clean farmer! Then she remembered how he had laughed when she splattered him with manure that morning (was it only a month ago?), so maybe he wasn't too clean. June was starting to realize that all the farms were sort of on display for each other. New Yorkers did the same thing when they dressed to go out—they were strutting their stuff with the clothes they wore. A neat farm was a chance to show off a little bit, and it would be nice to come home to this gleaming pair of rubber boots instead of the mud-caked pile strewn across Aunt Bridget's back porch.

She started up the back stairs and reached for the kitchen door.

She heard the sound of footsteps behind her.

"Stop!" It was Joe. He wasn't really shouting, but he was whispering as loud as he could.

"What are you doing here?" June asked, whispering back even though there was nobody else around.

Joe shrugged. "I parked the tractor down the road," he said.

June looked hard at him. "Then you're in?" she asked.

"Okay," he said nervously. "But we can't go inside the house, June. We really can't. That's breaking and entering."

"What's to break?" June asked, pulling open the kitchen door. "Nothing's locked."

"Nobody locks up around here unless they're

going away on vacation," said Joe. "You can't just walk into places."

"Well then, what do you suggest?" June let go of the door, which banged shut. Joe jumped at the sound.

"Let's just look in the windows," he said. "See what we can see."

June looked doubtfully at the house. The windows were too high to look inside without a ladder, and there was a whole second story. "We could look in the windows from the porch, I guess," she said. "But then we can be seen from the road."

"Climb up on my shoulders," said Joe. "Come on, quick. I can walk around every side but the porch, and you can look inside."

"What if it's right there inside the front room?" asked June.

"Better do the porch last," Joe said uneasily. "That way if anybody stops to ask, we can play dumb. It's not so suspicious to be on the front porch."

"What's really suspicious is taking someone else's Penny Book!" June said, hands on hips.

"Okay, okay! Let's get this over with." Joe crouched down so that she could grab his hands and climb onto his shoulders from the back-porch steps.

Joe was a little tippy at first, but then he found his balance and they started at the back of the house. They got caught up in some bushes but managed to push their way to the closest window.

"It's his bedroom," June whispered. "Maybe it's on his night table. . . ." She quickly scanned the room. Just like the rest of the farm, the room was in perfect order. The bed was made with a green plaid bedspread, and there was absolutely nothing on top of the bureau or on either bedside table. "Nothing," June said. "Let's go to the next one."

"This is wrong," murmured Joe, but he picked his way through some more shrubbery to the next window, which looked into the back of the dining room. Inside was a dark brown oval table, polished and gleaming, with portraits in small oval frames on the walls. There was a sideboard with an empty glass dish that looked like it was supposed to hold glass fruit.

"This is the most boring house I have ever seen," June said.

"Come on!" Joe said, shifting from one leg to another. "You're getting heavy!"

Next were the kitchen windows, which were slightly higher for some reason, but June grabbed the sill and pulled herself up to peek inside. It was harder to look into the kitchen because there were small checked curtains covering half of each window, but there was an open newspaper on the table.

"At least he's human," June said.

"What?" asked Joe. "You see something?"

"Evidence of life. Go to the next ones."

"These are the last two," Joe said. "Must be the pantry."

"Okay," June said, and grabbed the sill closest to her so that she could see past the large holly bush blocking her way. "Ouch!" she yelled as one of the spiky leaves cut into her hand. She started sucking her finger where the blood seeped out.

"Hurry!" said Joe.

June pulled herself up, bloody finger and all, and

scanned the room. High shelves were filled with Mason jars and canned goods. A pile of material sat on the counter in a box marked "Rags," and June rolled her eyes. This guy probably kept count of his dust mites. Then her eyes widened. On the highest shelf of the pantry there was a gap in the rows of Mason jars—and there it was, a fat spiral notebook.

"Joe!" she yelled, letting go of the sill and sitting back hard on Joe's shoulders. "I found it! The Penny Book!"

"Don't move so fast!" Joe yelled, but he was teetering, and June clutched at the sill as he began to fall backward. They both crashed into the holly bush and fell out onto the lawn just as Bob's truck came to a halt at the top of the driveway.

20
Trespassing

"What! Why—what is going on here?"

Bob stood over them, dumbstruck. June and Joe scrambled to their feet.

"I'm sorry," June began. "We were just . . ." For once she was completely out of ideas. How could she explain why they were peering into Bob's windows? Bob's eyes were popping out of his head. She tried again: "I— We— It's all my fault—"

"We were being nosy," Joe said, looking Bob straight in the eye. "I apologize, Mr. Burgess, but it's the truth. We were poking around where we shouldn't have been."

"You certainly should *not!*" said Bob, looking from one to the other as if he was still unsure that these two children were actually standing in his perfect yard, at the side of his perfect house, where it looked as if nothing ever happened that wasn't planned well in advance.

"It's all my fault," June said again. "I wanted to see what your house looked like, and Joe was just helping me—"

"Helping you?" Bob glared at her. "If you want to see my house, you knock on the front door and ask permission to come inside and have a visit! I don't know about New York City, but that's how we do things around here." He seemed to have caught his breath, and now he turned on Joe. "I must say I am surprised at you, Joe. And I'm afraid I'm going to have to call your mother."

"Yes, sir." Joe looked at his feet. June had never seen anyone look so ashamed since Indigo was first being housebroken and made a few "mistakes."

"I will be calling Bridget as well," Bob huffed at June. "You've caused a heck of a lot of trouble, you know."

June opened and closed her mouth without protest. The main thing was that Bob not find out they knew the Penny Book was here. That part still didn't compute, but she would figure it out later. Now she knew where it was, and that Bob (for whatever reason) had decided to keep it. Nobody kept things headed for the This 'n' That shop on the highest shelf in the pantry.

"Yes, sir. I am sorry, sir." She tried to look as contrite as Joe.

"And stop calling me sir!" he thundered. "I'm not your teacher; I'm your neighbor!"

"Yes, sir," June said without meaning to.

Bob threw up his hands. "Just don't do anything," he said to them both, which of course was what they were already doing. Bob checked around the roots of the holly bush for damage. Joe and June looked at each other, and June wondered how much it cost to replace a holly bush if it was ruined forever.

Bob slowly stood up, brushed the dirt off his hands, and turned to look at the house. "You kids find anything of interest looking from the outside?"

"No, sir," said Joe.

"No, Mr. Burgess," said June.

"You may find it more interesting to come in the front door and wait in the living room while I call your people."

He started around the side of the house toward the front porch. June mouthed "I'm sorry" silently at Joe, who shrugged without even the ghost of a smile. They followed Bob up the front steps to meet their doom.

June was scared of how angry Aunt Bridget would be, but Joe looked truly miserable. June could have kicked herself. Of course Joe had been right all along! She kept trying to apologize and take the blame, but when Joe's mother spoke to him on the phone after Bob called, Joe quietly agreed with everything she said. After he hung up, he asked if Bob thought Aunt Bridget would mind bringing him home.

"My mom wants me back right away," he said to Bob. "I'll drive the tractor home tomorrow, after the chores are done."

June looked from one to the other. Chores? What chores?

"You can count on a full afternoon here," Bob said to Joe.

"I'll come right after school," Joe said. Bob nodded without saying anything. In fact, nobody had said much after Bob made the necessary phone calls. June was afraid that if she tried to apologize again it would only make things worse.

The old black-and-white portraits stared at her sternly from the wall above the sideboard. There was a woman wearing a high-collared shirt, with her hair pulled straight back, who looked only slightly less friendly than the man in the frame next to her. At least he had a large mustache that curled up at both ends, though he wasn't exactly smiling for the camera. June didn't have to be told that Bob's people would not have appreciated anyone spying on their descendants. She tried not to keep looking at the doorway that led into the kitchen and the pantry beyond, where the Penny Book was waiting for her.

If only she had some kind of magic spell to get the book to fly off that high shelf—and while she was at it, she might as well give herself powers of invisibility or she'd never get away with it. The family portraits scowled as if they could read her mind.

The arrival of the old pickup that never left the farm broke the silence; it was so loud, it sounded like a motorcycle. Aunt Bridget entered without knocking and immediately started in on June.

"I ask one thing of you." She glared at June. "Only one thing on one day, and this is what happens?" June and Joe both kept their mouths shut. Bridget looked at Bob, who was sitting in his chair with hands clasped, nodding at everything she said. "I am so sorry, Bob. Trespassing on your property!"

"Well, I wouldn't call it trespassing, exactly—" began Bob.

"What else is it called when you make yourself

at home on somebody else's land without permission?" Aunt Bridget snapped, and turned back to June. "And what about decorating for the Halloween dance? Was that just another story to get into some other kind of trouble?"

"I *did* have to decorate——" June began, but that only gave Aunt Bridget more fuel for the fire.

"You better have, because I am going to check up on that with Ms. Huff! Don't think that I won't!" Now she turned to Joe. "And you! You've got the reputation of being a good, steady boy, Joe Pye. I must say I am shocked, and I'm sure that your mother is as well."

"Yes, ma'am," Joe murmured, his face turning so red, it matched Bob's suspenders.

"It was all my fault——" June began, but Aunt Bridget held up her hand and June stopped, knowing it wouldn't do any good.

"Well!" Aunt Bridget stopped to draw breath and looked at all three of them as if she was simply beyond words. "Well. Well!"

"Well, indeed," said Bob fervently.

June kept her eyes on the carpet.

"Have you discussed the punishment?" she asked Bob.

"We discussed it, yes," said Bob, looking at Joe. "They can come over and do some chores after school tomorrow."

"After school! How about June arrives here at six a.m. and gets to work before she gets picked up for school!"

"Bridget—" Bob began.

"Sunup to sundown! That's what I say," Aunt Bridget continued, glaring at June.

"Fine with me," June said. "I don't need to go to school."

"Now, now." Bob held up his hand before Aunt Bridget could say anything. "I think that after-school chores are a good way to learn their lesson. They won't do it again."

Aunt Bridget opened and closed her mouth, looked at Bob, then June, and finally, Joe.

"Very well," she said. "You will start here directly after school. I don't care if you're supposed to decorate the whole darn town for Halloween!"

"Yes, ma'am," said Joe.

They all looked at June.

"Yes, Aunt Bridget," June said.

"You can set them to chores for the rest of the week if you like," Bridget said to Bob. "Make a list!"

"I'm sure one day will be enough," Bob said. "There's always plenty to do around here."

June thought despairingly of Bob's perfectly trimmed hedges and how bad she had been at cutting the hair of her dolls and stuffed animals when she was little. (More than one had ended up with an accidental Mohawk.) If she was lucky, maybe he would let her shovel the manure out of the pens. She had gotten pretty good at that over the past month.

Aunt Bridget was right: she had been getting into trouble ever since she got off the plane. And now she had gotten her one and only friend into hot water as well. But there was a very good reason for everything she had done except for the biggest thing of all—ending up here in the first place.

It was a silent ride in the pickup to Joe's place.

June kept hoping that Joe would look at her and forgive her, but he stared out the windshield with his lips pressed tightly together. June sat squeezed between the two of them, dreading being alone with Aunt Bridget and wondering what kind of tasks she would have lined up for June as punishment once she got home. Plus, she had missed her chance to get the Penny Book back. Why did Bob have to come home just when she found it! June stared glumly at the road ahead. It seemed like nothing was ever going her way in South Dakota. They passed the entrance to the dump, and June was surprised when they pulled in at a sign for the state park.

"You live here?" she asked. Joe nodded. "Cool!"

Joe looked out the window. "Yeah," he said without enthusiasm. "We're the third campground on this loop," he said to Aunt Bridget, who drove right past the unattended entrance booth. Bridget stopped in front of a pop-up camper that was all set up with a blue tarp strung over a picnic table, a camp stove, and a large container of drinking water. A stream ran past the campsite, and there was a fire pit with a metal grate across it and tree-stump chairs in a circle. It was a very pretty spot, though June noticed that there was no car parked in front, and this was the kind of trailer that needed to be towed.

"This is great, thanks." Joe reached for the door handle.

"Joe—" Aunt Bridget put her hand on his arm to stop him. "It may not look like it, but winter's nearly here."

"I know," Joe said quietly. "Don't worry, Miss Andersen, we always move back into town before it gets real cold. Mom's got it all figured out."

"Well . . ." Aunt Bridget looked hard at Joe, and again that word seemed to have a world of meanings. June looked at the lit-up camper windows, hoping for a glimpse of Joe's mother, but there was no sign of life. "All right," Aunt Bridget said at last, letting go of Joe's arm. "I'll see you tomorrow at the Burgess place."

"Yes, ma'am." Joe opened the door quickly. "Thank you for the ride."

Joe hurried inside the camper, and Aunt Bridget

pulled past the other campsites, all of them empty. It was nearly dark now, and without any campfires or other people around, it felt a little spooky.

"Is it safe to live out here?" June asked as they pulled back onto the main road.

Aunt Bridget didn't answer right away, and June was afraid that she had made another misstep, but when her aunt replied, her voice was quiet. "Safe enough," she said. "I don't think anyone's going to bother them, if that's what you mean. I'd rather be out in the woods than lots of places."

"But nobody's camping out here but them," said June.

Aunt Bridget kept her eyes on the road. "There's camping and then there's living. Joe and his mother aren't on vacation; they live there. You know that."

"But why?" June asked.

This time her aunt did turn to look at her, but now she looked more sad than angry. "It's not just in made-up stories and faraway places that people fall on hard times, lose their jobs, have to move— happens right here in Red Bank, and I'm quite certain it happens in New York City." Aunt Bridget pressed on the gas, and the old truck lurched forward. "There's worse places than out in the woods," she said again.

When June arrived at Bob's farm the next day after stopping at home to change into work clothes and pick up Indigo, Bob was sitting on his front porch, reading the paper. June was wearing a clean flannel shirt and had pulled her hair back into a ponytail, hoping to give the impression of a hard-working sixth grader instead of a small-time burglar. If she worked long and hard enough, maybe Bob would change his mind about how much trouble she was. If Bob changed his mind, maybe Aunt Bridget would too. But most of all, she wanted Joe to forgive her.

"Hello, Mr.—Bob," June said politely from the porch stairs.

Bob looked up from the paper. "Joe's already in the barn," he said. "I made a list of some chores."

"My aunt said that she's expecting me home by dark," June said. "But I can walk home from here."

"Radio said we might be getting first snow tonight," said Bob, looking at the horizon. A slow-moving bank of gray was overtaking the high blue sky. Bob shaded his eyes and scanned the clouds. "We'll see if that's snow or rain when it gets here. If it hits before you leave, I can drive you both home."

June wondered how there could possibly be a snowstorm on the way. It was only October and a perfect fall day. She jumped off the last step of the front porch with Indigo at her heels. Joe was halfway under a tractor inside the barn, and when she kicked his feet hello, he grunted.

"What are you doing?" Indigo scooted under the tractor and started licking his face.

"Hey, cut it out!" Joe said to Indigo, who ignored him and kept snuffling at his ear until Joe pushed him away. "I'm changing the oil on the tractor—that's first up on the list." He sounded kind of cranky.

"Oh," said June. "Need help?"

"Not really," Joe said. "It's almost done."

"Where's the list?"

"In my back pocket. I'll be done in a minute."

June looked around the barn, which couldn't have been more different from Aunt Bridget's. This barn was clean and freshly painted. All the stalls were empty except for a pigpen, with a large black pig lolling inside a doghouse with its snout poking out. The pigpen led outside, and she saw two smaller pigs at the trough.

It was hard to connect these solid, living creatures with bacon and eggs on Sunday morning. June had read that some cultures thanked the animals for giving up their lives before eating them, and even though she didn't eat bacon, she leaned way over the railings of the pigpen and said "Thank you" to all three of the pigs.

"What are you doing?" asked Joe. She hadn't heard him come up, and he and Indigo were both staring at her.

"Thanking them for the tradition of Sunday breakfast," she said. "Not for me, but on behalf of the species: humankind to porcinekind."

"Porcinekind?"

"Porcine just means pig. It's a great Scrabble word. 'Porcinekind' I just made up, so you couldn't use it in Scrabble, but it sounds pretty good, don't you think?"

Joe looked confused, but with Indigo right there she thought it best not to explain too much about gratitude to porcinekind, though Indigo didn't seem to look at barnyard pigs as relatives any more than June thought every human being on the planet was her first cousin once removed.

"What's next on the list?" June asked, to change the subject.

"You know how to paint?" Joe asked.

"Sure," June said. "I love to paint! I took

Saturday classes at the Art Students League."

"Okay," Joe said slowly. "There's some cans of paint set out. You can paint the chicken coop while I fix some fencing."

They picked up the paint, rags, and brushes, and headed over to the coop, which was a neat little shed set off from the barn with wire fencing around it.

"Doesn't look like it needs a coat of paint," June said dubiously. The chicken coop was as neat as everything else on the farm, with a rooster stenciled in white on the little red door.

"That's how he keeps everything looking so nice," Joe said. "You don't want to wait till it's peeling to get to it."

June gave a small sigh. Joe was a bit of a know-it-all on the farm, which was annoying even if he *did* know it all compared to June. She had already decided that the next time she tried to get the Penny Book from Bob (which would somehow be today), she wasn't going to tell Joe. She didn't want to get him into any more trouble.

"Ever been inside a henhouse?" Joe asked.

June shook her head.

He opened the little door, and there was vigorous fluttering as a couple of hens skittered out to the chicken yard. The coop was well ventilated with small windows along the roof that were hinged, propped open, and screened with chicken wire.

There was a row of hay-filled nesting boxes on either side of a central aisle that led to a narrow plank and a small hatch leading outside, where the plank continued down into the chicken yard. It must work like a drawbridge, June thought. You just pulled up the plank and closed the hatch when the chickens went to bed. A miniature chicken castle.

Joe picked up a wire basket hanging on a nail by the door and handed it to June. "Check the nests for eggs."

June wasn't sure exactly how to do that, but she took the basket and boldly put her hand right into the first one. She fished around with her fingers, hoping that chickens didn't poop where they slept. She felt something hard and a little bit warm, and when she pulled it out there was an egg! It was smaller than the ones from the store, mostly brown with a little speckling of white.

"Holy Saskatchewan Sunday," June breathed, holding it up for Joe and Indigo. "A real egg!" Indigo reached out his nose for a sniff.

"I'll bet you'll find a few more," Joe said.

June put her hand into the next box—nothing, the next one—nothing, but then in the third one she came up with two! They were all slightly different shades of brown, and she placed them very gently in the wire basket. "They taste better than store-bought," Joe said. "But your aunt probably has chickens too."

"She does," said June. "But I haven't collected any eggs yet."

"Don't tell her how much you like it, and maybe she'll let you do it every day." Joe grinned at June despite himself. "You finish up with the egg collecting and I'll set up the paint and brushes."

June went slowly from box to box, and she collected not only eggs, but feathers as well. There were gray-and-white-spotted ones, reddish downy ones in a tight curl—and stuck in the wood next to the hatch she saw one perfect tail feather from the rooster in an iridescent green arc.

June and Joe worked all afternoon. Joe patched the wire fence that went around the vegetable garden. June cleaned and painted the inside of the chicken coop roof. The temperature was dropping as the afternoon wore on, but June didn't mind the chores. Painting was fun because things looked better right away, and she liked watching the chickens; she made up names and stories about each of them. She wanted to tell Indigo, but when she looked for him, she found him curled up in a nest box, probably dreaming of omelets.

Joe finished up a little before June, and Bob said it was all right for him to leave since he had started earlier. Joe had told his mother that he would loop back into town for groceries before coming home.

"It takes a while on the tractor," Joe said to June, who was still painting the chicken coop. "Guess I'll see you in school."

"Right," June said. She hadn't mentioned the

Penny Book to Joe all day, but she wondered if he was thinking about it too, sitting right there on the pantry shelf. She had hoped that Bob would give Joe a ride home. Then she could sneak in and grab the book, but now that wasn't going to happen. Joe was looking at her with a funny expression on his face.

"What is it?" she asked, already feeling guilty about even thinking about stealing from Bob.

"I'm not really going grocery shopping," he said. Now *he* was the one looking guilty.

"You're not? Where are you going?"

"Back to school."

"School? How come?"

Now Joe didn't only look guilty; he looked a little mischievous. "I want to hand in a story about the Halloween dance for the paper. If they take it, maybe it'll be my first article."

"First article!" June repeated loudly.

"Sshh!" Joe said, though Bob was back on the porch and couldn't have heard them.

"That's great, Joe!" she whispered.

"Might as well try," he said, scuffing his sneaker on the grass. Then he looked right at June and smiled.

"I bet they *will* take it." June crossed her fingers and held them up so Joe could see.

"Thanks," Joe said. Indigo nudged Joe's leg with an encouraging snort, and June waved her paintbrush good-bye, splattering paint on the back of one of the hens. Luckily, it was a white one, the same color as the paint. She and Joe started laughing. "I don't think Bob will notice," Joe said. "Call you later."

"Call you later," said June. Joe walked off toward his tractor, which had spent the night by the side of the road. This must be what kids who went to school did all the time. June didn't like school or homework, but she definitely liked the "call you later" part.

June washed out her brush and put away the paint cans, rags, and brushes in the barn. She still didn't have any idea how to get the Penny Book, and once Joe left, it was impossible to think about anything else. She had to come up with a plan. Since she'd eaten ice cream for breakfast, taken a ride on the La-Z-Boy express, and traveled inside a beehive, nothing else had happened. She knew that the metal that won't stick to a magnet had to be the Big One, and it seemed pretty clear by now that the list was all about Red Bank, but that was as far as she and Indigo had gotten. Once she had both the list and the Penny Book in her hands, she was pretty sure that the two of them could figure out what happened to the Big One. She always kept the list in her pocket and had been tempted to tell Joe about it every day and see if he had any ideas. But now that they had gotten into so much trouble about the Penny Book, she was definitely keeping it a secret.

June made her way up the steps to let Bob know that she was all done, Indigo trotting beside her. It was getting colder and Bob was wearing a woolen cap with ear flaps, though he still sat in his rocker with the paper on his lap.

"I'm all done, Mr. Burgess," she said.

"Bob," he said. "I mean it—everyone calls me Bob."

"Bob," she said hesitantly. "I finished painting and put everything away."

"Good," he said, eyeing the horizon. "Let's hope the rain holds off so it will dry faster."

June shifted, not sure how to excuse herself. She could walk home from Bob's place, and it was almost supper time. She could hear Indigo's stomach growling from here.

"Would you like to come in for a minute?" Bob asked. "I've got something I'd like to show you."

June's heart leaped. The Penny Book! She followed him inside and he led the way into the kitchen. She pulled out a chair, trying not to look at the shelf in the pantry. Bob poured her a glass of milk and put out a plate of cookies with agonizing slowness.

She took a big gulp of milk and slipped one of the cookies to Indigo as Bob walked into the pantry and reached up to a high shelf. But instead of bringing down the Penny Book, he picked up a large jar of pennies and set it on the table with a smile.

"This is my coin collection from back when me and your mom collected together," he said. "I thought you might like to have it."

June stared. The only penny she really cared about was the Big One, and there was no way she could ask him about that without giving everything away.

Bob sat down opposite her, looking a little concerned. "I hope you don't mind," he said. "I don't really have any use for it anymore, and you seem interested in coin collecting, so——"

June remembered her manners. "No! No, I love it," she said, reaching for the jar and holding it between her hands. "Thank you so much, Mr.—— Bob." She looked up at him. "It's so kind of you to give this me. I really appreciate it."

"Your mom and I spent a lot of time collecting together," Bob said. "She was always the ringleader, of course, but I didn't do so bad myself."

"When did you stop?" she asked. "Did you——" She took a deep breath. "Did you ever find any really valuable coins?"

"Not really, no," Bob said. "Your mom had a knack for finding the most valuable ones. I just liked to collect them." He looked at June with a strange expression she couldn't read. "And spending time with her, of course."

"You were best friends, weren't you?" June asked.

"We were." He looked a little sad but smiled gently. "You look quite a bit like her, you know."

"I don't think so," June said, kicking at the legs of her chair. "She had red hair, and mine is so boring."

Bob laughed that big, infectious laugh she had heard at the barn when she threw manure on him by mistake. June giggled without even knowing what was so funny, and all of a sudden she could imagine why Bob had been her mother's best friend. He must have been fun when he was a kid.

"Your mom wasn't a natural redhead." Bob leaned forward as if somebody might overhear him. "I don't know if it's all right to tell her secrets to you now, but I remember when she started dyeing it that color. She had just turned sixteen."

"Really!" June was stunned. Her mother had always looked so glamorous with her red hair and cool sunglasses.

"Oh, yes," Bob said, still smiling. "When she was a little girl, her hair looked a lot like yours, which is very pretty, by the way."

June shrugged and turned the jar of pennies around in her hands. It was heavier than it looked.

"You can open it," Bob said.

June knew the Big One wasn't in there, but Bob looked at her so expectantly that she opened the jar and tipped some pennies out onto the kitchen table.

Bob ran his fingers through them, then picked one up that was particularly darkened by sweat and age. He checked the date. "Now, this one isn't worth that much money," he said. "But I can tell you about the day that I found it. Your mom and I had stopped to get something at Kleinsaasser's Drug Store. They had a counter where you could get Cokes and lime phosphates and Green Rivers."

June had no idea what those last two things

were, but she didn't want to interrupt him.

"Everyone stopped there after school. I remember on that day we were exactly one cent short for a couple of soda pops, and the guy who owned the place didn't like kids very much, so he never cut us a break. We were mooning around, looking at the menu (which we knew by heart, of course), and Roseanne saw the edge of this very penny sticking out from the bottom of one of those red spinning stools they had at the counter." He laughed again. "Your mom was so excited. It's a 1974, see?" He held it out to her so she could see the date. "We never got the phosphates, because your mom made me save this penny to trade out for another one from the jar the next day. She said it was our lucky penny. From then on whenever we had to pick a number, you know, for math class or a game or something, your mother always said, 'Seventy-four!' It used to drive our teachers crazy. They'd ask us to pick a number from one to ten, and your mom would yell out, 'Seventy-four!'"

He passed the penny to June. She looked at it,

imagining her mom with dark brown hair and a best friend named Bob.

"Did she get into lots of trouble at school?" she asked.

"A bit of trouble," Bob said. "But everyone loved Roseanne. She was always full of plans and ideas. The whole Penny Book project was her idea. I was lucky she liked to hang around with me, though it could be just because we grew up next door to each other."

"Can you remember something about every penny in here?" June asked.

"Oh, I doubt that," Bob said. "That's a lot of pennies and a lot of years. But I do remember some things." He shrugged. "You don't have to keep them all, June. You can take them down to the bank and get some of those paper coin rollers and turn them in for pocket money if you'd like. I don't mind."

"No!" June surprised herself with how vehement she sounded. "I like to think about you guys collecting together," she said more quietly.

"Okay," Bob said, scooping up the rest of the

pennies and putting them back into the jar. "These are yours to keep."

June thought of something. "Can we keep them here?" she asked suddenly.

Bob looked at her. "Sure, but—why would you want to do that?"

"Maybe . . ." June hesitated and Indigo whined, looking up at her face. He knew her better than Bob did, but June rushed on without looking down at him. "Maybe I could come by again, you know, hear some more stories about my mom."

Indigo whined loudly and she nudged him with her foot to be quiet. Indigo knew what she was really thinking: it would give her a good excuse to come back to the house and take the Penny Book when Bob wasn't looking. How did Indigo always know everything?

Bob looked surprised but happy. "I'd like that very much," he said. "Anytime you want to come over, you're more than welcome."

"It'll be kind of like a game," June said brightly, feeling like a terrible person as Indigo's whine turned into a sort of low growl in his throat.

"It certainly will," Bob said, a big smile lighting up his face. "A memory game." He seemed about to say something else, and June thought she saw his eyes flick to where the Penny Book was sitting on the shelf behind her, but she couldn't be sure. Indigo growled even louder and Bob looked down at him.

"That little pig is ready for his supper, I think," said Bob. "We'd better get you home."

He got up and put the jar on the counter near his tins marked "Flour" and "Sugar." "But it's your collection now. It'll be right here waiting for you."

Bob gave June and Indigo a ride home, since it looked like it was about to thunder, and in fact the sky opened up with rain just as they started up Aunt Bridget's driveway. Bob came inside to wait it out, and Aunt Bridget insisted that he join them for supper. June managed to avoid being alone with Indigo until Bob went home and she was headed up to her room to do homework. Once she shut the door to her bedroom and plopped him onto the bed, Indigo gave her a long, hard look.

"Oh Indigo, I'm not *that* bad," she said. "I do like hearing the stories, and he likes telling them. And if I get a chance to get back what *belongs to me* . . ." She stared him down. "There's some reason Aunt Bridget wanted to get rid of the Penny Book, and there's some reason that Bob isn't taking it down to the This 'n' That. I know it has to do with the Big One."

Indigo raised his eyebrows.

"Okay, I'm not one hundred percent sure. But think about it, Indigo. Traveling in the beehive and the La-Z-Boy express were both about meeting Moses—and now Moses is making sure that the Penny Book will come back to me if Bob drops it off like he was supposed to. So that means my mom wanted me to meet Moses *and* go to the This 'n' That shop. Aunt Bridget is the one who knows about ice cream for breakfast, so Mom wanted me to meet Aunt Bridget so that I could find out what she did with the Big One, especially if Aunt Bridget's the one who ripped those pages out of the Penny Book! The Big One was probably on one of those missing pages, Indigo, don't you get it? Maybe even the page she wrote the list on!"

Indigo looked a little skeptical.

"Do you have any better ideas?" she asked, a little annoyed. Indigo thought for a minute, then slowly shook his head.

"I'm going to get back Mom's Penny Book, Indigo—I don't care what it takes! Come on, let's take one more crack at the list before bed."

She pulled it out of her pocket and spread it flat on the bedspread for the hundredth time.

"Here's what's left," she said. "Now think!"

J.S. 2 R.B. 4 B.D.

"June Sparrow plus a some weird numbers and letters. Do you know numerology, Indigo?"

Indigo shook his head.

"Me neither," said June. "I don't even know what it means, but we've got to crack the code! Here goes:

Climb a ladder to the top of the world
Hug my oldest friend
Find metal that won't stick to a magnet

Indigo looked up at her.

"Okay, we know what that last one means, but we still haven't found the Big One, so I'm keeping it on the list," she said. "When we cross that off the list, we've got our ticket out of here."

Indigo sighed and put his head down on his front trotters.

June read the last item out loud: "'Let gone-byes go bye-bye.' That's a weird one. I've heard of bygones, but not gonebyes. Maybe it means the same thing, kind of like a clue in a scavenger hunt. What do you think?" Indigo's long eyelashes were shut tight. "Indigo?"

Indigo had apparently decided to go bye-bye himself.

June reached under the bed and felt around for her purse. She checked that her birthday penny was still inside, along with her mother's old driver's license. Then she checked the numbers on the license, just in case they matched up to J.S. 2 R.B. 4 B.D.

No such luck. None of it made any sense.

June shoved the purse back under her bed.

"I just want to find the Big One and bring us back home," she said, snuggling up to Indigo. "I know we can do it. We're going to find the Big One and go straight back to New York, just like my mom did."

Indigo nuzzled her cheek. He knew she sounded braver than she felt.

22
Silo

Over the next several weeks, June got into the habit of stopping by Bob's place, picking pennies from the jar, and hearing stories about her mom. She liked hearing the stories, and despite the fact that it was all part of her master plan to get the Penny Book when his back was turned, she had to admit she liked spending time with Bob, even if he was a grown-up. Thanksgiving was coming, and Aunt Bridget was planning on having everyone over for a traditional dinner. She had invited Bob and Moses along with Joe and his mother. Aunt Bridget seemed to be looking forward to hosting, even though this meant that she was even grumpier than usual. She went over the menu every morning, though June didn't think that turkey giblets were exactly breakfast conversation.

The best thing about Thanksgiving was that it meant June wouldn't have to go to school for two whole days that week. She had made no progress with the list or with stealing the Penny Book. Now that she'd started having cookies and milk with Bob on a regular basis, going into the house when he wasn't home didn't feel as easy as it had before she knew him, and besides, Indigo didn't approve.

They let everyone out of school early on the Wednesday before Thanksgiving, and when June got off the bus, she decided to go over to Bob's place instead of straight home. Indigo was waiting for her down at the end of the driveway as usual, wearing a red plaid dog coat June had found for him at the This 'n' That. He thought it made him look country. June didn't have the heart to tell him that *nothing* made Indigo Bunting look country.

"Let's go to Bob's first," she said to Indigo. He loved going to Bob's, as it always meant cookies before dinner. June was trying to get into the holiday spirit, but she knew that Aunt Bridget would be in a state. As soon as June got home, her aunt would start her chopping celery and cleaning counters that were already spick-and-span. June tossed her schoolbag behind a bush at the end of the driveway and picked up Indigo. He licked her ear in the cold. "I know, Indigo," she said. "I should try to be excited about Thanksgiving."

They both sighed.

In New York it was their favorite holiday. They always watched the Thanksgiving Day parade from their windows at the Dakota. The huge balloons floated right by their windows at eye level, Clifford the Big Red Dog and Mr. Potato Head. They'd be watching the balloons get blown up in person tonight if they were still in New York, June thought with a sigh. Aunt Bridget planned to watch the parade on television as they cooked, but the thought of this only made June more homesick than ever.

Whenever June was thinking hard about something, she found it helpful to take a walk. Back in New York she could cover many blocks thinking as fast as she was walking, and she kept going over the list as she walked along the road to Bob's place. She still thought the Penny Book must have some hints to help her to crack the code, and she was certain there was a way to get the Penny Book if she could only hit on the right idea. Bob's truck was in the driveway, but June walked past the house toward the barn. She wanted to keep thinking just a little longer.

There was a gleaming metal silo towering next to the barn with a tall ladder leading up the outside that she hadn't noticed before. Perfect! She could climb up to that slot on the roof that was open like an observatory to the sky and think things through. What really mattered when she was searching for a solution to a problem was simply changing the view. There must be a great view from the top of the silo, she thought, as she stared up at the metal rungs. Joe had explained to her that the open slot in the silo roof was where farmers filled the silo up with grain, and there was a door at the bottom to collect the stored grain as needed through the winter. But it was a lot more fun to pretend the roof was open to the sky so that an astronomer could observe the wheeling of the stars.

That's when it hit her:

Climb a ladder to the top of the world.

"Indigo! This is it!" June shouted. "The ladder to the top of the world!"

She grabbed the ladder and started climbing as fast as she could. She didn't know what she'd find at the top, but every step brought her closer to the Big One and going home! Indigo wanted to come with her and whined anxiously, but she couldn't carry him up without a backpack.

"I'll be down soon," she called back, a little shocked at how far away the ground looked already. "I'm just going to look at the view!"

This didn't seem to reassure Indigo, who began

circling the bottom of the ladder, but June kept going. She had never been afraid of heights and she hoped to learn to mountain climb someday. She had taken some beginner classes at climbing walls just for the fun of it, and she loved the ropes, the special knots, and launching herself into the air from one toehold to the next on her way back down.

The silo was higher than it looked, and when she finally reached the silvery roof and looked back down at Indigo, he appeared very small, even for a miniature pig. I'll just stay a few minutes, she told herself, and climbed up the last few steps so that she could peer inside.

For some reason, she hadn't expected the silo to be full of grain, or maybe it was just that she hadn't expected it to look so vast. It was like a huge well filled with grain instead of water, deep and wide. She turned back to look at the view and the farmland spread before her like a quilting pattern with the tree breaks as stitching. The houses looked tiny, clustering together in Red Bank, then scattering again just past the edge of town.

"Indigo!" she yelled as loud as she could. "I did it! This is the ladder to the top of the world!"

June's words were whipped away in the wind, and she couldn't tell if Indigo heard her or not. She hadn't really thought about the wind, which picked up as she climbed and seemed even stronger now that she was at the top. It blew her hair around her face and into her mouth, but she didn't want to take a hand off the ladder to brush it aside, so she turned her face directly into the wind and tried closing her eyes halfway. She could see better this way, and she felt the silo swaying like a mast on an old-fashioned sailing ship far out at sea. The sky had turned a solid gray that wasn't so solid when you really looked at it, and there was an elemental taste in the air that made her wonder if Aunt Bridget could be right, there might be a Thanksgiving snowstorm.

Turning back toward the silo, June saw a small metal platform just inside the opening, like a bridge leading from one side of the silo to the other. Maybe her mom had climbed this very silo when she was a kid, and that's why she wrote it on the list. Maybe there was even a clue about the Big One inside! June climbed onto the platform, but it was pitch-dark except for the bar of light from the opening. Her own shadow fell across the wide circle of grain in front of her.

"Lordy, Lordy Liberace," she swore.

"Liberace!" the silo echoed back. Even though the wind was whistling across the opening, the inside of the silo was like an echo chamber. She let go of the ladder and moved carefully to sit on the edge of the platform and dangle her feet. The air was so still inside the silo, it was almost as if there was no air at all, and she had to look at the opening in the roof to remind herself that there was, in fact, plenty of air. But the light from the opening was filled with dense particles of dust, which might be why it was so hard to breathe. Dust was whirling up from the grain in tiny circles, and June tried not to give in to the eerie feeling that she had just stepped into the den of an ancient troll who gathered grain like gold.

"Saskatchewan Sunday!" she called louder.

"Sunday!" the silo echoed back, and June giggled nervously.

The silo giggled nervously.

I wonder what kind of grain this is, she thought. It definitely wasn't corn, though Bob had a huge cornfield stretching out behind the barn. If you thought about it in a certain way, this whole part of the country was like a Russian nesting doll with squares inside of squares. Starting with the square of the farmhouse, then the yard, then the fields. A geometric pattern repeating itself all the way from the Mississippi River to the Rocky Mountains.

June leaned down to pick up a piece of grain and taste it. But the grain was farther away than it looked—and suddenly June lost her balance, falling right into the silo on top of the mountain of grain. At first she thought it was kind of funny and was glad nobody had seen her do something so klutzy. But when she reached up to get back onto the platform, the slippery grain gave way before her arms like water. Kicking her feet to move upward, June suddenly felt the grain sucking back on her legs, and she sank even deeper. Her heart froze. The slick kernels of grain worked like quicksand, and June did what you are never supposed to do in quicksand—she panicked.

"Help!" she screamed as loud as she could.

"Help! Help!" echoed the silo.

June gave a huge wrench with her arms, and her fingers grazed the underside of the platform, but then she sank back even lower. The platform looked farther away, like she was looking up at sunlight from the bottom of a pool. She thrashed desperately, sinking quickly down to her armpits. Now she started crying, and the silo echoed back her sobs like an evil genie. June shut her eyes and spit out the grain that had gotten into her mouth. She sank down another inch. That was when it started to snow. The inside of the silo went even darker as the first flakes began to blow straight inside with the wind.

"Help!" June yelled again, but her voice sounded strangely hollow. "Indigo! Help!"

The wind was whining across the narrow

opening of the silo, and she knew there was no way that anyone would hear her up there. What if she never got out? What if she never saw Indigo again? Would Aunt Bridget turn him into bacon when she wasn't there to protect him?

"Indigo!" she called again as she slipped down a little farther.

She tried to remember what they had told her in swimming class: never panic in the water; rest in a floating position. But how could she float when she couldn't lift her legs? Every time she moved, it only got worse. She could still hear her own voice calling distantly, "Indigo! Indigo!" but it was only the echoing silo.

I don't want to drown! she thought desperately, trying not to move, but when the grain got up into her nose she started thrashing again, spitting and choking. There were spots in front of her eyes now and she could hardly breathe, terrified that this time she might not come back up. Her lungs were bursting, but she couldn't stop trying to swim to the surface even though a part of her knew that struggling only made things worse.

June Sparrow was drowning in the middle of a snowstorm.

Suddenly she felt an excruciating yank on her scalp. She looked up and saw Bob on his knees on the platform, pulling her up by the hair. She felt nothing but pain at first. Then his hands were under her armpits, and the sucking sensation gave way as he pulled her up next to him and wrapped his arms tightly around her.

"It's all right," he said, his voice shaking. "You're safe."

She took great big gulps of air and Bob patted her back, holding her up like a rag doll. Then he moved her in front of the opening so that she could breathe the clean air, dense with white flakes and a sharp cold that stabbed her lungs. She still couldn't get her breath, and she was gasping, crying, and coughing all at once. Every breath she took felt like swallowing broken glass. Bob turned her around to look at her. She had never seen him look so scared.

"You all right?"

June nodded—she couldn't speak. She was still taking deep, gulping breaths.

"Okay," Bob said. "We're going down."

June never really remembered how they got down that ladder. She was aware of Bob's big body between her and the snowstorm, and his voice encouraging her to keep moving one foot then one hand, one foot then one hand, as they slowly descended the narrow ladder, which seemed to have grown even longer, like the magic beanstalk that grew as high as the sky in "Jack and the Beanstalk." Once they made it to the ground, Bob scooped her up in his arms and ran for the farmhouse.

The next thing she remembered was being on his couch with a blanket over her and Indigo madly licking her face and hands as Bob made her drink a huge glass of water and a teaspoon of whiskey. She coughed hard, burst into tears, and this time she thought she'd never stop crying.

23
Roseanne

"It was your little friend here who saved you," Bob said, looking at Indigo. "I heard him scratching at the door when I saw the first snow flurries, but he wouldn't come into the house. He kept pulling me over to the silo." Bob's voice was shaky, and the white stripe between Indigo's eyes was furrowed with worry. "He wouldn't quit till I started climbing up. Never occurred to me that you'd go up there."

June hugged Indigo hard. She had settled down after Bob got her a large box of tissues and made a pot of tea along with the usual plate of cookies. Bob hadn't called Aunt Bridget yet, and June wondered if he was as reluctant as she was to tell her aunt what had happened. "I have to tell you that was lucky," Bob said quietly. "About four people die a year in silo accidents. Fall in and drown, just like that."

June shivered and Indigo snuggled up even closer. It was very strange to have just escaped drowning and still be bone-dry. Bob looked at her again, and she knew she owed him an explanation. He didn't look angry, and she realized he must have been just as scared as she was. Then she realized something else—Bob had saved her life.

"Thank you," she said. Bob shrugged and looked at Indigo.

"He's the one to thank. That's one smart little pig."

June pulled Indigo close and kissed both of his ears. He knew what she meant.

"I'm sorry," she said to Bob. "I just—I had this big problem and I was looking for a place to think. I didn't know it was so dangerous."

"It's my fault. I should have told you not to go up there." Bob shook his head. "I keep forgetting you're not from around here. You look so much like your mother, and you know all the trouble she used to get into. She used to climb silos too, though I don't think she ever fell in."

"That's what my problem is! I mean—" June's throat was sore and it was hard to talk, but this was too important. "Not *her* getting into trouble, but *me*! The only reason I keep getting in trouble is because of her."

"What do you mean?"

"I mean the Penny Book," June said, deciding to come clean no matter what the consequences. Bob had saved her life and she owed him the truth. "Her Penny Book that talks about you. The one that you have right here in your pantry."

Bob stared at her. "How did you know that?"

June flushed. "Me and Joe were looking for it when you caught us looking in the windows. I'm sorry, I'm really sorry! But I found it in Mom's closet. Then Aunt Bridget took it, and she said you had taken it to the This 'n' That shop, and—"

"And it wasn't there, so you came looking for it over here," Bob finished.

June nodded. "I'm very sorry about spying on your house," she said quietly. "I know it was wrong, and I got Joe in trouble too."

Bob got up from his armchair, and June figured this was it. He was going to call Aunt Bridget, and June would be put into South Dakota Chore Jail for the rest of her life. But instead of going to the phone on the wall in the kitchen, Bob walked right through to the pantry and reached up to the highest shelf. He pulled down the Penny Book and walked back to the living room. He placed it in June's lap without a word.

"It rightly belongs to you," he said quietly. "I shouldn't have kept it after Bridget told me to take it down to the drop box, but she was going to get rid of it, and I couldn't see that as right either. I didn't know what to do with it. I'm the one who owes you an apology, not the other way around."

June stared at the notebook in her lap, then up

at Bob. He was clasping and unclasping his hands, looking down at the rug as if he didn't want to look her in the eye. And suddenly it hit her: he was still in love with her mother and had been for all these years. It was kind of awful and sad, but also terribly romantic and tragic—just like *La Bohème*.

"Have you looked through it?" June asked. Bob shook his head.

"Let's look together." June moved over on the couch so that Bob could sit next to her, and they started flipping through the Penny Book. Bob laughed at some of the entries. He knew much more about each of the pennies than Roseanne had written down.

"Do you have a Penny Book?" June asked.

"No," Bob said. "I got rid of mine when your mom left town."

There was a silence. It seemed so sad to get rid of your Penny Book.

"Did you guys ever go to New York?" June asked. "I mean, before my dad came along."

"No, we never did." Bob sounded a little sad as

well. "I should have listened more to your mom, that's for sure."

"What do you mean?"

"Your mom always dreamed big. Just like she says right here. She didn't want to spend the rest of her life in South Dakota, and once your dad came along, well . . . , the rest is history."

"The rest is history," repeated June. They had come to the entry about being handed a penny by a boy named Jimmy, and the torn-out pages at the back. June closed the book, hoping that Bob hadn't seen the part about her father, but she knew he had, and she impulsively reached out and patted Bob's big hand. He started a little in surprise, but he didn't move away.

"How did they meet? My mom and dad? I mean, how come he came to Red Bank at all?"

"They met at the Vaudeville Palace," Bob said quietly. "That old theater in town that's all boarded up now. Back then it still showed movies, and your mom worked in the box office on weekends. Your dad was driving from California, and I guess he wanted to take a break and catch a movie. I think it was *Grease*."

Grease! thought June. No wonder her mom had the album on her record player. It was their movie!

"Jimmy took one look at your mom, and, well—I think he decided she was a girl worth sticking around town for, which she certainly was. . . ."

"That was it?" June asked. "He just stayed on after he met her?"

"Jimmy got a job working at the Vaudeville Palace so he could date Roseanne," Bob said. "He dreamed big, just like your mom, but he hadn't made it big yet. He stayed in town for about a year. He worked concessions and she sold the tickets. Then, after she graduated high school, they got married and lit out together for the Big City."

June knew better than to let Bob know how absolutely perfect and romantic this was.

"What happened to the Big One?" June asked quietly. "It was a 1943 copper, wasn't it? Struck in copper?"

Bob stared at her without saying anything.

"Do you have it?" June asked. "Is it glued onto one of the missing pages?"

"It *was* a 1943," Bob said. "Struck in copper. Very rare, but she found it and we authenticated it. It was the real thing and worth a lot of money, even then."

"Where is it?" June asked urgently, still patting his hand as if he was a big, scared child.

"I—I . . ." Bob looked her in the eye. "To tell the truth, June, me and your mom parted company over that penny. I wish that wasn't the case, but—well—" Bob took a deep breath. "I asked her to marry me and save that penny for a nest egg to someday buy a farm of our own, kind of like this one."

June blinked hard and Bob kept talking. "But I was just the boy next door. We never even went on an actual date. She always said we were only good friends, but I guess I kept hoping. I figured she wouldn't take me seriously unless I asked her to marry me, so I did, even though we were still in high school."

"Really?" June breathed. "I mean, I know she was young when she had me, but I didn't know she had already been proposed to twice!"

"She was quite something, your mom," Bob said, smiling again. "But by the time I worked up the courage to pop the question, she had just met your dad, and we could never agree about how to spend the money from the Big One, so—"

"So?"

"So she went ahead and cashed it in for something she really believed in."

"What?" asked June, not sure she wanted to know. Had her mother blown all the money on a fancy wedding dress?

"Your father," Bob said. "She believed in him, and even though she told me that he didn't want her to cash it in either—guess that's why they kept working at the Palace—in the end I figure she must have changed his mind, and they used it for that invention of theirs, Sticky Glue. We all thought it sounded crazy, but it turned out to be a gamble that worked out well—for all of you."

"Really?" June said. "They spent the Big One? Are you sure?" She and Indigo locked eyes. It couldn't be true. The Big One couldn't really be gone!

"Absolutely," Bob said. "She told me they had gotten married and she was cashing it in, and I'm afraid—I'm afraid we had a fight over that too." He shook his head and looked down at the Penny Book across their laps. "It is nice to hear her voice again in here, though."

"She spent the Big One," June repeated, as if she had to try to make herself believe it. "She spent it, and now the company it started is bankrupt."

"That penny was spent a long time ago," Bob said.

"Numismatics Corporation," June said slowly, the empty feeling inside getting bigger. "It must be why they named it that, even though it was a stationery company."

"I guess you're right," said Bob. "Honoring the penny that got it all started in the first place."

Now I'll never get out of here, June thought

miserably, but she didn't have the heart to say this to Bob. It was more obvious than ever that he'd never gotten over her mother.

"There's some other things in the box your aunt gave me," Bob said. "I'm not sure if they belonged to Roseanne, but if they did, maybe you'd like to have them."

June nodded dumbly, and he headed back to the pantry. It was snowing hard and starting to get dark outside. The wind had picked up even more, and June looked out the window at the storm—blizzards were something she'd have to get used to now that she was going to be stuck here forever.

Indigo looked up at her from where he was nestled in her lap and gave her a gentle nudge with his snout. "I know, I know," she whispered to him. "At least we're both okay. I could have died in that silo." She and Indigo both shuddered and she clutched him even tighter. "It's just—I'd been hoping for the Big One, that's all. But you're right, Indigo. The main thing is that we're together." He rested his head on her knee.

Bob came back with a big cardboard box and set it on the rug in front of her. "Not sure why Bridget felt she had to get rid of these things," he said slowly. "But if there's anything you want to hold on to that you can't take home, you can always store it here."

There was an old alarm clock with a brightly colored flower appliquéd on the back that looked like her mother's style. There was a teacup missing its handle and a key ring with a logo from Mount Rushmore, and some loose papers lying flat against the cardboard bottom. June turned these over and saw her mother's handwriting. She quickly started scanning them.

"These are the missing Penny Book pages," she said. "Why do you think—"

She stopped speaking. At the very top of a ripped-out page, in her mother's flowing script were the words:

I'm pregnant and nobody here understands, not even Bridget. Especially Bridget! I'll never

forgive her for what she said about Jimmy—
This is the worst day of my life. Give it up for
adoption—

There were some more words scratched out so
June couldn't read them. The only words June cared
about were crashing over and over in her brain: *This
is the worst day of my life. Adoption.*

24
Snow-Blind

June was out the door before she had time to read
it twice. Bob yelled after her but she couldn't hear
what he said, and she didn't stop to find out. She ran
for the road with Indigo squealing in her arms, the
afghan from the couch flapping around her shoulders in the dark. *Worst day of my life* and *adoption*
kept ringing in her ears all the way down the lawn,
under the fence, and out onto the road, which she
hit at a run.

She slipped on the new snow but kept running

as if she would never have to stop. The cold air was slamming into her chest, and snow filled her sneakers. She heard a car coming behind her and ducked down into the ditch so that she couldn't be seen. Maybe it was Bob looking for her, but she didn't care. She didn't care about anything—she just wanted to get away. It had been so easy to pretend that her mother was perfect, marrying a dark handsome stranger and pursuing her dreams. A baby was supposed to make everything even *more* perfect. And not just any baby, June thought angrily—I'm the one who made it the worst day of her life. June clambered back up onto the road once the car went by and stomped right past Aunt Bridget's driveway. Indigo was utterly still, so even he must be a little scared. She didn't know where she was going, but she certainly wasn't going back to her mother's old bedroom.

June stumbled and almost slipped down into the ditch, and then it hit her. It really was dark and cold out here, and she had better figure out something pretty fast. Maybe she could go into the state forest and stay with Joe and his mother, just for tonight. She wished she had his mother's cell phone number, then remembered that she didn't have a cell phone herself, so it wouldn't do her any good.

"Okay, then," she said out loud for courage. "We'll just keep walking till we get to Joe's place." Indigo whined nervously, and she pulled the afghan tighter around them both. The snow was getting thicker, and from the look of things there hadn't been any snowplows yet. Finally June saw a green sign off to the right. It was half covered in snow and too dark to read, but she figured it must be the sign for the park. She wondered how far up the road the campground was, then remembered the little booth at the entrance. "We can stop to rest there," she said to Indigo. "It's not too far to Joe's campsite."

If Joe's mother was as nice as he was, June hoped she wouldn't mind if a snow-covered girl showed up at their door, but honestly, June had stopped caring about anything except getting inside somewhere, even just the entrance booth of the state park, before they froze to death. "Drowning and freezing all in the same day!" she said to Indigo, and started laughing, but Indigo didn't join in with that silent, shaking laughter that she knew so well. "Welcome to South Dakota!" she yelled into the swirling flakes around them, and realized she was getting kind of giddy. Could this be hypothermia? She couldn't tell if the numbness she felt was from the weather or the shock of finding out that her mother had never really wanted her in the first place. If her mother had wanted to give her up for adoption, what did it matter what happened to her now? She laughed again in the dark, and Indigo made a growling noise in his chest the way he did when he thought danger was near. "Oh, be quiet, Indigo," June said impatiently. "I'm fine. We're fine!"

But they weren't at all fine, and June began to slow down as they continued up the hill in the dark. She wondered how far they had come from the main road. She thought they would have reached the entrance booth by now. What if she couldn't find Joe's campsite? Just then she saw a light flickering on and off up ahead, and she started pushing toward it. She didn't know what it was, but she knew that she and Indigo had to get to shelter. As they got closer, she saw that the light wasn't really flickering—it was a steady glow from a window, and waving tree branches were making the light unsteady. But that light was getting closer with each step.

She smelled woodsmoke and began to think about a fireplace and hot cocoa and what it would feel like to be warm again. As she got closer to the light, she noticed that there were lots of strange shapes around her, half covered by snow. Squares and tubes that looked like boxes and pipes were scattered on the ground. The road narrowed to a pathway winding around all these hidden objects, and she had to be careful not to trip over anything. She passed a car without any windows, slowly filling up with snow. She was so tired that she almost gave in to the impulse to crawl inside and go to sleep on the front seat, but the yellow light and smell of woodsmoke beckoned her on.

"This is a strange place," she murmured to Indigo, as she passed what looked like an empty refrigerator, and she thought she heard the sound of someone playing the violin. At this she began to think that she must be hallucinating from the cold, but the music didn't stop even when she told herself that it was all in her head. She vaguely wondered if it was coming from the house with the yellow window, but who would leave their refrigerator outside? And could that black cone on her left really be a huge pile of car tires tilting over like the Leaning Tower of Pisa?

She stumbled the last few steps toward the light, and the music got louder. She saw the door to a little cabin and thought to herself that this was a strange hallucination indeed, for it looked just like the cabin built onto the back of Moses's truck. If this was all a mirage brought on by hypothermia, June was past caring. She couldn't feel her feet anymore, and Indigo was wriggling inside her shirt, digging his trotters hard into her stomach to keep her from collapsing in the snow. She walked up to the door of the cabin and knocked hard.

It opened wide and there was Moses, sitting in

his wheelchair, violin in hand.

"June!" It really and truly was Moses. She didn't know how or why, but it was Moses and this was his truck with the cabin on the back. He stared for a long moment, as if he couldn't believe it was June, then reached out a hand to help her clamber up inside the cabin without asking any questions. He plopped her into an armchair in front of a glowing woodstove. She sat like a wooden doll as Moses pulled off her shoes and socks, then rubbed her bare feet with a towel until they started to tingle. Then he took a lump of beeswax that smelled like menthol and rubbed her feet and ankles hard before putting them into a pan of warm water that hurt at first, then felt like the loveliest bath she had ever had the pleasure to enjoy.

The scent of honey and mint filled the cabin as Moses went back and forth, wrapping her in rugs and blankets. Indigo wriggled as close as he could to the fire, wrapped in another blanket that Moses tucked around his shoulders. All this time Moses didn't ask any questions, and June didn't need to do anything but watch as he bustled around the cabin, which was decorated floor to ceiling with hand-woven rugs from the shop. Her brain was so tired and her heart was so wounded that she couldn't make sense of anything anymore. She didn't think she would ever feel strong and brave again. Moses pressed a mug of hot soup into her hands and put a small bowl in front of Indigo, who lapped hungrily. June took a sip and felt her insides expand with gratitude. It was her favorite: chicken soup with rice.

"Where are we?" she asked when she finished her first mug and he filled it for a second time.

"This is the town dump," Moses said. "This is where I live."

"I thought this was the road to the state park! I was looking for Joe."

"That's a bit farther down the road," Moses said, and she could tell he was worried. "Good thing you turned in here."

"And you play the violin?" June asked. "I thought I was only imagining . . ."

"Not the violin," Moses said; "the fiddle." He

took the instrument back out of its case and picked up the bow. He began to play the tune she had heard outside in the snow, and it sounded familiar though June couldn't imagine where she had heard it before. It sounded as haunting and comforting as firelight itself, and she and Indigo listened as their bones warmed up and the steam rose off both of them in the flickering light from the woodstove, where the logs shifted next to each other and embers glowed below.

Finally, June began to talk. Moses's eyes widened when she told him about the silo accident, and they widened some more when she told him about what she had seen written in her mother's Penny Book.

"I'm not going home tonight, or maybe ever. I can't, Moses. I can't be in that house anymore." She finished and there was a long pause as they both looked into the fire. For the first time in her life, June didn't see dancing figures in the flames. She only saw logs burning away into ash.

"You can stay here tonight," Moses said. "But we

have to go to your aunt's house and tell her where you are. She must be worried sick about you in this storm, and I don't have a cell phone."

"Do we have to?" June began, but one look from Moses made her stop. She knew he was right. "All right," she said. "Thank you for letting me stay here."

"Nice thing about having your home on the truck is that you don't really have to go out to leave home," Moses said. "You sit right here while I drive over there."

"Okay." June was feeling sleepy now, and she couldn't imagine going back out into the storm. Indigo couldn't even open his eyes.

She pulled her chair up next to a fold-down table that latched up onto what looked like a real tree trunk built into the wall, with a couple of small branches sticking out. There were two coffee mugs and a few tiny ornaments hung on the branches, sort of like a combination cup holder and Christmas tree. There was a heart carved in the center of the tree trunk. June leaned in closer. Inside the heart were two sets of initials: "R.A. + J.S."

June looked once, looked again, and then looked up at Moses.

"J.S.? Those are my initials."

"They're also your father's," Moses said. "Jimmy Sparrow. Roseanne and Jimmy were married right here in the truck on New Year's Eve, almost thirteen years ago."

"My parents? You knew them? Why didn't you tell me before?"

"Your mom always loved making up riddles. I figured she wanted you to figure out the riddle of Red Bank on your own. I've been waiting for the right time to tell you, and I guess that's now."

June reached out and touched the heart. "They got married here? Why?" She stared at her parents' initials. It all seemed like a dream.

"I'm licensed to marry folks," Moses said simply. "Another one of my sidelines. People around town know that, and every few years a couple comes along that wants something different from a church wedding. Your mom wanted to be married inside a beehive with all that sweetness around. They got married right here in the truck, just about where you're sitting, as a matter of fact."

June didn't say anything.

"They loved each other," said Moses. "They got married for love and for life. And I'm pretty darn sure they were hoping to have children someday."

June forced herself to ask, "Then why did she write that in her Penny Book, Moses? How come?"

"I don't know," he said. "But I do know they loved each other, and I know they loved you too."

"But I don't," June said very quietly. "I don't even know them anymore. Not really."

"Sometimes we don't get to know everything all at once," said Moses.

June wouldn't look at him. Sometimes we never get to know anything, she thought.

"Let's go up to your aunt's place so she doesn't worry, and then we can get back up this hill before the snow gets any deeper." Moses reached for a hook at the back of the cabin and unlatched a small door that led directly into the cab of the truck.

"What's that?" June asked.

"Another special feature," Moses said. "Since I live in the back of the truck, I got them to cut a door in between the front and the back so that I can hitch myself back and forth without having to go outside. I keep one chair back here and one chair behind the driver's seat."

It was pretty ingenious, and Moses transferred himself from his wheelchair to the front seat by pulling up on a couple of handles on the ceiling. But for once June watched without saying anything. She couldn't think anymore about great inventions and initials and mysteries. She just wanted to get it over with, then come back home with Moses and fall asleep in front of the woodstove. Moses reached down to swing his legs over to the other side, then pulled the little door shut behind him. She heard him settle into the driver's seat and start the engine.

June wanted to close her eyes, but she couldn't stop looking at the initials carved into the wood in front of her.

Everybody knew her parents but her.

25
Birthday Penny

Strangely enough, nobody was home at Aunt Bridget's house when they pulled up. The Cadillac was there and the lights inside the house were on, but nobody was home. June left Indigo inside and ran back out to the truck. Moses looked worried.

"She's probably out looking for you," he said.

"But the car's here," June said. "Maybe I should just leave a note."

"You can't just leave a note when people are out looking for you in the snow," Moses said firmly.

The wind had dropped a bit but the snow was still falling steadily, and the sound of Moses's truck was muffled even though June was standing right next to it.

"Look at those tire tracks." Moses pointed to the driveway. "She must be out looking with Bob Burgess. Listen, June, they may be out for a little while, so I'm just going to pull off down the road past the bottom of the driveway, where it's flat. You wait for them inside, and after you explain things to your aunt, come down and we'll go back home together. I don't want to leave the truck on this incline. Not good for Floyd."

"Isn't he—they—asleep?" June asked doubtfully.

"Sure are, but we all sleep better when we're flat out." He smiled at her. "Don't worry, I'm not going to leave you. Just getting down off this hill before I get stuck in the snow."

Moses slowly drove the truck back down the long driveway, the lights from the little cabin tilting as he bumped along. June ran into the house, where

Indigo was waiting for her in front of the gas heater. She put her hands out toward the blower and realized her sneakers were dripping onto the rug. She carried them upstairs to see if she could find some dry clothes in her mother's closet.

It didn't feel the same walking into the bedroom now that she was determined to leave. She threw her wet clothes and shoes in a pile and grabbed a dry shirt and pair of jeans out of her mother's bureau without caring what they looked like. At least there were plenty of pairs of dry socks, and she layered on two, just in case. In the back of the closet was a pair of red cowboy boots with white piping that would probably fit, but June didn't allow herself to admire them. Nothing that belonged to her mother felt good anymore.

She grabbed one of her mother's suitcases from the closet and started to pack her things. Maybe she could borrow enough from Moses for a bus ticket to New York. She would go to her favorite places and find a way to sleep there. She would sneak into the stacks at the New York Public Library or sleep inside the Great Canoe at the American Museum of Natural History. Anywhere but here. She pulled her fancy dress off a hanger in the closet and reached under the bed to grab her purse. It was still lying open from the last time she'd looked in it, and the case with her birthday penny skittered across the floor. Indigo ran to pick it up for her, and June heard a sharp crack as he grabbed it in his mouth. Indigo spit the hard plastic case out indignantly, and two pennies rolled out onto the floor.

Two pennies. Not one.

June stopped packing. There must have been two pennies, one stacked on top of the other, inside the broken case. Why did her mom do that? June picked them up. One was the 1965, but the other one had a wheat design on the back; only the older pennies had that. June turned it over and stared at the date: 1943. Her hand started shaking. Bob had told her that her mom had cashed it in to start the company!

June pulled open the drawer of the night table, where she had seen a small horseshoe magnet along with a magnifying glass, some paper clips, nothing special. Now she got it—these weren't random items; her mother had them next to her bed for a reason. June took the magnet out of the drawer, hardly daring to breathe, and held it up to the penny. It didn't stick. It was copper. She took out the magnifying glass and looked at the date again: 1943.

This was it. The Big One.

She turned to Indigo, who was staring at her as if he already knew.

"I found it," she whispered.

"We've got the 1943. It's for real, Indigo. We can go home!"

Indigo leaped into her arms and started licking her face madly. She giggled and they rolled around on the bed together, the 1943 penny clutched tightly in her hand. She sat up and stared at the penny again as Indigo ran circles around her on the bedspread. It had been right there in her purse the whole time! Her mother hadn't cashed it in after all! She didn't know what had really happened, but June Sparrow was never going to give up this penny until she sold it to the highest bidder.

"The *real* Dakota, here we come!" she said to Indigo.

Suddenly she remembered the list, and pulled it out of her pocket.

J.S. 2 R.B. 4 B.D.

"J.S.," June said slowly. "Just like in Moses's truck . . . it could be June Sparrow *or* Jimmy Sparrow."

"And 2—two—the two of us, maybe? 2 R.B.—*two* or *to*. But *to* what?"

June gasped. "Wait a minute, Indigo!" Indigo's ears were sticking straight up and his curly tail started to wiggle. "If it's *to*, not *two*, then it's *to* R.B.—*to Red Bank*! June and Jimmy Sparrow to Red Bank! Do you think that's it, Indigo?"

Indigo's tail was going in mad circles.

"To Red Bank 4—*for*—B.D.—*birthday*! That has to be it, Indigo! We figured it out! June Sparrow to Red Bank for Birthday! J.S. 2 R.B. 4 B.D.!"

Indigo squealed loudly.

"She wanted to bring us back to Red Bank for my birthday! She wanted to show me everything, Indigo! Moses's truck, the La-Z-Boy, ice cream for breakfast, even the silo!"

June turned over the piece of paper to look at the empty circle drawn in red marker. She gently placed the 1943 penny in the circle.

"A perfect fit," she breathed. "The Big One. But . . . but"—June looked at Indigo—"I still don't get it. If she wanted to give me up for adoption, then why—"

The door slammed downstairs.

June started to run for the stairs, then stopped. She didn't want Aunt Bridget or Bob to be worried about her, but she had to be careful with the information she'd just figured out. She didn't have to tell anybody she had the Big One. What if Aunt Bridget wanted to take it away? Or Bob thought half of the money belonged to him? And if her mother hadn't wanted to keep her in the first place, what was June supposed to think about any of this? She put a finger to her lips to warn Indigo to be quiet. He looked at her questioningly but followed as she crouched out of sight at the top of the stairs. She needed time to think things through.

"You sit," she heard Bob say to Aunt Bridget. "I'll get the whiskey."

Indigo and June exchanged a look. They had never seen Aunt Bridget drink before. Maybe it was medicinal, like the teaspoon Bob had given her after the silo accident. She heard glasses clink on the counter and liquid being poured, and it sounded like a bit more than a medicinal dose. June peeked through the railings at the top of the stairs. She couldn't see their faces, but she could see Aunt Bridget from the back as she sat in the armchair. She hadn't even taken off her rubber boots, and there was a pool of water gathering on the hearthrug in front of her, but for once she didn't seem to care. Bob came over with the whiskey and handed her the glass, patting her shoulder with his other hand.

Aunt Bridget took a sip, then leaned her head forward into her hands, and her shoulders started to shake. June couldn't believe what she was seeing. Bob patted her shoulder. "She'll be fine, Bridget. I'm sure she's indoors somewhere by now."

"You think I'm just going to sit here?" Aunt Bridget sobbed. "When that little girl is out there in the snow? If anything happens to her, I just—I don't know what I'll do, Bob. She's so much like Roseanne, it felt like my second chance."

June couldn't take it anymore. She started to her feet, but there was a knock at the door and Aunt Bridget sprang up. "Maybe it's the police!" she said.

The police! June sank back into her hiding place. She was going to be in more trouble than she ever thought possible. She clutched the penny tightly. Would they even let her leave the state?

Aunt Bridget opened the door and there was Joe, snow on his hat and jacket, and he was pushing Moses's wheelchair.

"Is she here?" Joe asked. "After you called, I drove the tractor all around the state park. Then I came here and saw Moses parked down near the bottom of the drive, so he followed me up here in his truck." Joe's eyes were wide as he looked from Bob to Aunt Bridget.

The wheels on Moses's wheelchair were covered with snow, but unlike Joe, Moses had a smile on his face. "Everything all right now?"

"Moses!" called June, and she tore down the stairs, unable to take it anymore. But instead of landing in his arms, she found herself in Aunt Bridget's, who held her as if she would never let her go. Aunt Bridget was crying and everyone was talking at once and Indigo ran circles around all of them, curly tail sticking straight up in the air.

26
Let Gonebyes Go Bye-Bye

After the police had been called, and June had been scolded and hugged by Aunt Bridget, they all settled around the big gas heater in the living room with mugs of hot cocoa. June hadn't had a chance to tell them everything that had happened, but it was enough for now to see how happy Aunt Bridget was to have June home safe. Looking around the circle of faces, June realized that she had to tell them about her discovery. She caught Moses's eye, and as if he knew she had something momentous to say, he held up his hand for quiet, and everyone looked at him, then over at June as he nodded at her.

June took a big breath and fished into her pocket for the penny, where she had been touching it every few minutes to be sure it was real. She held it out for them to see. Then she pulled her mother's magnet out of the other pocket and held the penny up to it. It dropped from the magnet into her palm. Bob and Joe gasped, Moses grinned even wider, and Aunt Bridget looked confused, glancing from one to the other.

"Is this one of your and Roseanne's pennies?" she asked, turning to Bob.

"If that's what I think it is, it's only Roseanne's," Bob said in a reverent voice. "But how?" He held out his hand. "May I?"

June nodded and handed it to him, and Joe practically jumped out of his chair to look over his shoulder. Bob whistled low and long. "So she never did sell it after all," he murmured. "I wonder . . . I wonder . . ."

"It's the real thing—1943?" Joe's voice cracked

as he stared at the penny shining in the center of Bob's broad hand.

June nodded. "It's the Big One, Joe."

Joe shook his head in disbelief and Aunt Bridget looked a bit annoyed. "Will someone please tell me what's going on?" She sounded more like her old self, and June grinned.

"My mom found that penny thirteen years ago," June explained. "We thought it was gone, but . . ." She looked at Bob, who carefully handed it to Joe. Joe held the penny up to the light as if he was looking at a rare diamond, and June gave him the magnet. "But I found it again tonight, and it turns out"—she looked at Aunt Bridget—"I think that my mom meant to give it to me all along. And . . ." She paused. "This penny is worth a whole lot of money."

Moses had a sober look on his face, and he caught June's eye with a questioning look. She stopped talking and looked down at Indigo, who gazed up at her from his warm spot in her lap. He looked so comfortable there, like he was home at last.

June took a moment to look around the circle.

Bob was looking like a big shaggy dog with sad eyes but happy all the same. Joe had his mouth partly open, still stunned by the find. He kept holding the magnet to the penny and watching it drop. Every time it fell into his hand he gasped, then did it again. Aunt Bridget looked confused, but she waited for June to finish what she had to say. Finally June turned to Moses, who gave her a look as long and deep as the night she had been through. She knew that whatever she said next, he would understand.

"So it looks like I'm rich again," June said slowly. "Maybe not quite as rich as before, but a lot richer than I was when I got here. It's enough money for me to go back home."

"Before you say anything else," Aunt Bridget said with a loud sniff, "I owe you an apology."

"What for?" asked June.

"Bob told me that you saw Roseanne's Penny Book today." She held up her hand before June could protest. "It's all right. It belongs to you."

June looked at Bob, who gave her an encouraging nod.

"But what I'm most sorry about," Aunt Bridget continued, "is that you read those torn-out pages. I tore those pages out years ago because I was ashamed of myself. I was trying to hide an old quarrel between your mother and me. I guess it's no secret that we were all a little shocked when Roseanne and Jimmy ran off and got married." Here she gave Moses a look. "And then you came along right after they were married. You were a honeymoon baby—"

"A honeymoon baby?" June stared at Aunt Bridget.

"Roseanne and I might not always have agreed about everything. After all, I was the one to bring her up after our parents died. We were just a couple of teenagers when we lost them, so when Roseanne eloped at eighteen, then announced she was pregnant—well, I thought she was too young for all that responsibility." Aunt Bridget took a deep breath. "Your father left town on a business trip right after they found out she was pregnant, and I hate to admit it, but I didn't trust him to come back for her. I told her to give you up for adoption—"

"*You* told her—"

"I was wrong!" Aunt Bridget looked helplessly at June. "I've never been more wrong in my life! I was only nineteen myself, but Roseanne never forgave me. That's why we never talked after she left town. That's why she never came to visit. But you have to know that she *always* wanted you and loved you."

June dug into the pocket of her jeans and pulled out the list. She unfolded it carefully and looked at the rest of them.

"I think that my mom *was* planning on coming to visit," she said. "I think she was planning to come visit with me."

Aunt Bridget's eyes filled with tears and she put a hand to her mouth.

"All of her favorite things to do in Red Bank were written on a page she tore out from the Penny Book all those years ago." She looked at Moses. "That's how I know she wanted to come back home."

June took a deep breath and began to read the list aloud:

"'J.S. 2 R.B. 4 B.D.' That part was the hardest," June said. "But I think me and Indigo finally figured it out: J.S.—June Sparrow, or Jimmy Sparrow, or both of us—2 R.B. 4 B.D.—to Red Bank for birthday." June took a big breath. "I think that this list was what she wanted to give me for my birthday, though I don't know which birthday she was planning on.

Travel inside a beehive
Climb a ladder to the top of the world
Hug my oldest friend
Eat ice cream for breakfast
Take a ride on the La-Z-Boy express
Find metal that won't stick to a magnet
Let gonebyes go bye-bye"

June stopped reading.

"I guess some of the things on this list aren't so hard to do if you live in Red Bank," she said slowly. "But I think my mom was planning on showing me all of them. I was so sure the list was going to lead me to the Big One, and that the Penny Book would explain everything once I got it back. But I was wrong about that. I found out something from the Penny Book that maybe I wasn't supposed to find out about. . . ." She looked at Aunt Bridget. "But there's still some things left on the list, and even though my mom's not here to do them, I think I can check them off for both of us." June hesitated, and Indigo nuzzled her elbow in encouragement.

"This one is for you," she said to Bob. "Hug my oldest friend." June gave Bob a big hug, and she could feel his face burning red in embarrassment.

Joe was standing right next to Bob, and on an impulse, June gave him a quick hug as well. "And you're my newest friend," she said simply. Joe blushed even brighter than Bob and pulled his cap a little lower, but June could see his smile.

Then she turned to Aunt Bridget. "And I think the very last thing on the list is for you. 'Let gone-byes go bye-bye.'" She held out her arms to Aunt Bridget, and this time they both started crying though neither of them had meant to. When they stopped hugging, June handed the list to Aunt Bridget, who stared at it in amazement.

June looked down at Indigo, who gazed steadily at her. "Indigo is my very best friend," she said slowly, "and Indigo and I have decided . . . even though we might be millionaires, and we miss the bright lights and the big city"—Indigo smiled up at her—"we think we would miss all of you even more. We've decided to stay right here for now."

Aunt Bridget gave a small shriek and kissed June, then each of them in turn. (June wondered how much whiskey Aunt Bridget had drunk to go this far!) But Moses was smiling broadly, and June went on, "I think that it would be nice to have Christmas here with all of you, and maybe"—she winked at Bob—"maybe we can put some of this money away as a nest egg, you know, for college or something, after we have a really special Thanksgiving feast."

It was the best Thanksgiving June had ever had.

The penny was worth even more than they had hoped, and even after setting up two college funds (one for Joe and one for herself), June still had plenty left over. She sent a large Christmas basket to the prison where Mr. Mendax was spending the next ten years, and an even larger one to Shirley Rosenbloom in Long Island City. But she decided that instead of lots of presents, she wanted to give everyone in Red Bank something that would last forever. So with Aunt Bridget's help she formed the Indigo Bunting Vaudeville Palace Fund to reopen the old movie house on Main Street, and Miss June Sparrow made such a sizable donation that it was able to open just before Christmas. Joe's mother was hired as manager, and it turned out that she *was* just as nice as Joe. The plan was for Joe's mom to work in the box office, Aunt Bridget would keep track of expenses, and June would run the concessions stand. June even got the Metropolitan Opera from New York to agree to put the Indigo Bunting Vaudeville Palace on their list of movie houses that would show operas onscreen, live from New York!

The first opera to come to town was *La Bohème*, which was beyond perfect, and June kept telling everyone, "Me and Indigo saw this opera the night we left New York, before *anything* had happened."

They all got dressed up to go downtown for the show. Indigo wore his top hat and June wore her black dress with pink tulle, just like on her birthday night at the Met. Joe's mother surprised them with an indoor/outdoor strip of red carpet that led from the curb to the door of the theater. Moses drove June and Aunt Bridget right to the front, and Bob snapped pictures of their arrival. The camera flashed constantly despite Aunt Bridget's loud protests that she hated having her picture taken. Joe was now officially on staff at the school paper, and he was covering the event. June and Indigo granted the paparazzi a brief interview, and it turned out that Moses loved to pose for the camera. Everyone in town was there. Even Mr. Fitzroy came (with Ms. Huff as his date!) and as they walked by, June pulled out a piece of paper, swiped it with Sticky

Acknowledgments

This book would not exist without the love and support of many people. I am grateful beyond measure to Erin Cox (agent extraordinaire), Rob Weisbach (the Boss), Alessandra Balzer (editor extraordinaire), Kelsey Murphy, Janet Frick, Renée Cafiero, and the whole team at Balzer and Bray, the Vermont Studio Center, the Wertheim Study at the New York Public Library, Fairleigh Dickinson University, the Scott family of Hillside Farm, Ruby Tyng, Eliot Schrefer, Donna Freitas, Rene Steinke, David

Grand, Martha McPhee, Sara Powers, Annik LaFarge, Jennifer Collins, Leslie Gat, Louis Begley, Kate Doyle, Tim Weiner, my mother, and all my sisters (you know who you are). I read the first chapter aloud to Amy Edwards and hold her spirit with me. A special thank-you to Ken Buhler and Rebecca Magid—Ken for creating a penny book and Rebecca for saying, "Mom, that would be a great idea for a book!" This one is for Ken and the girls, with extra thanks for the salted caramels Ken doled out whenever I finished a chapter. In every way, I have never had it so good.